AF489108

TILL UNDEATH DO US PART

Boris Bacic

Title: Till Undeath Do Us Part
Author: Boris Bacic
Copyright © 2021 Butterdragons® Publishing
All Rights Reserved

This is a work of fiction. Names, characters, businesses, places, events, locales, and incidents are either the products of the author's imagination or used in a fictitious manner. Any resemblance to actual persons, living or dead, or actual events is purely coincidental.

No part of this book may be reproduced or used in any manner without the express written permission of the publisher except for the use of brief quotations in a book review. This includes, stored in any retrieval system, or transmitted in any form by any means – electronic, mechanical, photocopy, recording, or otherwise.

Published by Butterdragons® Publishing
https://butterdragons.com

ISBN: 9789493229686 (ebook)
ISBN: 9789493229693 (paperback)
ISBN: 9789493287198 (trade paperback)
ISBN: 9789493229709 (audio book)

Cover Design by: Dazed Designs

Audio book narrated by Joshua Schubart

When the world crumpled
We all had to adjust
To pain and loss
To another world

Constantly fearing for our lives
Because of creatures
Because of humans
Such a harsh world

Suddenly, our lives changed
When compassion overrode fear
We should have known better
We should have known they lied

Now, we pay the price
Now… now, we hide
Safe from those who mean harm
I protect her with my life

She owns half of my soul
She owns all my heart
She is my world
Forever

by Helle Gade

Prologue

He forgot all about his own safety the moment he saw her in danger. Only one thing mattered then – saving her, even at the cost of his own life.

"Jesus, what a mess," Jack said.

He slowed the car down almost to a halt as he observed the street. A chain of crashed cars stood abandoned in the middle of the street, effectively blocking the road. People ran in panic, some out of the buildings and across the streets, others doing the opposite. Occasional gunshots and caterwauls resounded somewhere in the distance. A plume of thick, black smoke billowed up in the air from somewhere in the center of the town and reached toward the sky like a monstrous tendril.

"I'm not sure if this is a good idea, babe," Linda said.

Jack looked at her. Her eyes were wide, transfixed on the chaos outside. He stopped the car, but kept the engine running. He gripped the steering wheel so firmly that his knuckles turned white.

"We'll be quick," Jack nodded to Linda. "Just gotta grab some stuff from the pharmacy and we're good to go. Okay?" He gently put a hand on her thigh.

Linda put a hand over his. She was icy cold. Jack took a better look at her and noticed how pallid she looked. She was scared, and rightly so. Outside was a warzone. Jack spun the car around and then killed the engine. He wanted to be able to get out of the town quickly in case the need for it arose.

As the car's engine sputtered out of life, the sounds outside became a lot clearer. Some of the screams conveyed terror. Others seemed to communicate pure pain. Jack expected the chaotic sounds to die down, but they only seemed to intensify. He looked in the rearview mirror. A female reporter and a cameraman stood in front of the pharmacy. The reporter held a microphone close to her mouth and the camera was pointed at her, while her lips were moving as she spoke something. She was so calm, even with the ruckus around her. Why these people were focused on doing their jobs at a time like this, was beyond Jack.

"Do you wanna stay in the car?" Jack looked at Linda.

Linda shook her head timorously. "I'm coming with you," she said.

"Alright, hon. We'll be out of here in no time."

Jack opened the door and stepped outside. As soon as the door opened, the noises outside became deafening. Jack had to shout to Linda to hurry so that she would hear him. He strode on the sidewalk with Linda, holding a hand on her back and gently rushing her while also looking around the street for any unexpected trouble.

A teenager with a pistol ran out of an alley right in front of Jack and Linda. Jack instinctively jumped in front of Linda to shield her. The teen didn't even look at them as he continued running. Not a moment later, a middle-aged man ran outside the alley and dashed after the teen. The corner of his lip was contorted into a stroke-like grimace, and his fingers erratically contracted and extended as he sprinted.

The teen turned around, pointed the pistol at the man, and a loud bang echoed in the street. The man's head kicked backwards as blood flew out the back of his head, and then he fell like a ragdoll. Linda screamed. The teenager looked at Jack. He had a look of terror in his eyes. For a moment, Jack was sure that the kid was going to shoot him. Instead, he spun on his heels and continued running.

Jack looked down at the body of the shot man. A pool of dark blood had already formed around his head. He had a red hole in his cheek, and his eyes stared vacantly at the overcast sky.

"Oh, my God…" Linda wept into her hands.

"Come on, let's hurry!" Jack put his hand on Linda's back and nudged her forward.

It took him a moment to avert his gaze from the dead man. Jack wished that he had brought his rifle. Now that he thought about it, it was really stupid not to bring a weapon.

"Steven, we are standing in front of the library in Eugene, Oregon. It is absolutely chaotic here," the female reporter said just as Jack and Linda went behind her and entered the pharmacy, not caring that they were in the reporter's frame.

Entering the pharmacy gave them a moment of respite from the chaos outside. The interior was about as trashed as Jack expected it to be. Shelves were toppled over, with medications littering the aisles. Glass displays were shattered, with fragments of glass all over the floor. A crashing noise came from the other side of the place, followed by low shuffling.

"Stay here, Linda. I'll be right back," Jack said.

Linda nodded. Jack peeked down one of the aisles. There was a woman slumped with her back against the shelf, her head drooping toward her chest. Jack couldn't tell if she was unconscious or dead. He ignored her as he strode toward the aisle with the antibiotics. Most were gone, but there were some bottles strewn on the floor. He imagined that whoever was trying to hoard the medications swept the whole shelf into a basket, accidentally knocking some of them on the floor and not bothering to pick them up.

Jack grabbed four bottles of antibiotics, and went down the aisle, browsing the half-empty shelves for anything else he might find useful. Another loud crash came from somewhere outside this time. Jack instinctively turned his head toward the exit but couldn't see it from here.

Screw this. They had first aid at home. If things really got bad, they'd come back to town later. Jack put the bottles in his pockets and loped back to Linda. She stood near the door, cradling herself and looking around worriedly. When she saw Jack coming back, her shoulders visibly relaxed.

"Let's go," he said and opened the door for her.

"Roger. Roger!" the female reporter shouted at the cameraman.

The cameraman was staring at something on the left. When the reporter called him, he jerked his head back toward her with a confused look on his face.

"Focus the camera on me," the reporter chided him. "The sooner we do this, the sooner we can get out of here."

"Sorry," the cameraman muttered and decided to stay more focused.

Jack and Linda broke into a gait past the reporter just as she started speaking about the situation in the town.

"As I was saying, it is chaotic out here. People are killing each other without hesitation. Just three minutes ago, we saw a young man rip out an elderly woman's throat with his teeth. The government has sent in military forces in armored vehicles and—"

A shattering sound came from behind Jack. He spun around instinctively to see what was going on. It all went down so fast that Jack hadn't even registered what had happened until it was too late. A male figure slumped face-first on the concrete, just inches away from the reporter. The man had tiny fragments of glass in his hair and jacket, and when he looked up, Jack saw that where one eye should have been, a pointy shard of glass stuck out, blood oozing out of the socket and running down his face like a tear.

The man let out an incoherent moaning sound as he grabbed the shocked reporter by the ankle. The reporter screamed and kicked against the man, but he had a firm grip. He reeled her foot closer and sunk his teeth into her calf with an animalistic growl.

The woman screamed, and the cameraman, who had been standing still all that time, screamed with her. Blood poured from the reporter's leg. She dropped the microphone and hit the man on the head with the palms of her hands, but he didn't budge.

Before Jack could think about assisting the reporter, another figure jumped out of the darkness of the pharmacy and tackled the reporter like a football player, causing her to slam the concrete hard. This one was a young woman, maybe no older than eighteen. She had bedraggled, blood-crusted hair, and her clothes were caked in mud. A bone protruded from her unnaturally bent forearm, sticking through the skin, but she didn't seem to be aware of it.

As soon as the woman was on top of the reporter, she dove toward her neck. For a moment, Jack couldn't see what was going on, but then the woman slowly raised her head, a long strip of the reporter's bleeding flesh hanging from her mouth and stretching like a piece of cheese.

By then, the reporter's screams became a lot more violent, and she kicked and thrashed violently – to no avail. The man who had bitten her leg was now feasting on her thigh, taking bite after bite, exposing the cartilage and the femur of the leg.

Another figure jumped out of the pharmacy and fell on its knees next to the reporter. It started eating her shoulder. And then another one jumped out. This one was a young man with long hair. He looked at the reporter, and then his eyes fell on the cameraman, who had dropped the camera and started running by then. The man went after him.

Jack stared in shock as the group of people feasted on the twitching reporter. He wanted to move, but he couldn't. He wondered over and over how close he was to meeting the same fate inside the pharmacy. That thought made him sick to the stomach.

"Jack! We gotta go, come on!" Linda tugged Jack's hand, snapping him back into reality.

He finally unfroze and realized in terror what a mistake it was coming here. Screw the medications, screw the supplies, he and Linda had to get out of here right now. He spun on his heel, grabbed Linda by the hand, and jackknifed down the street. He ignored the elderly woman struggling with a young lady who pinned her against the wall and bared her bloodied teeth at her.

Three men stood in front of them, all covered in blood, letting out incoherent, animalistic sounds, their heads and fingers twitching uncontrollably. The path to the car was blocked. They were pacing around the street, looking nowhere in particular. One of them looked at Linda and let out a scream.

Jack pulled Linda into the alleyway from which the teen with the gun ran out earlier. He hoped to God that the alley wasn't a dead end as he ran with Linda through it. He jumped over the young man whose entrails were hanging out of his belly and splayed on the floor. Linda gasped and panted behind him, partly from fear, partly from exhaustion.

"Come on, Linda! We can't stop!" Jack urged her.

Behind them, primitive gurgling, growling, and hissing sounds followed, just a few feet behind, he estimated.

Oh, shit. Oh, shit, shit, shit!

Jack pushed Linda forward so that he could protect her from behind. For the split second that he looked back, he saw one of the men running after them. He didn't stop to confront the man – that person looked like he could overpower him easily.

Jack turned around and ran after Linda, who had just reached the end of the alley. She turned to wait for Jack. He wanted to tell her not to stop, but he was too focused on sprinting to be able to speak. He practically collided with her when he reached the end of the alley, and then pushed her to keep running.

A woman ran past them, and suddenly, the caveman-like sounds from the chaser distanced themselves. Jack dared to stop and turned around to see the attacker diverting his attention to the woman. He would have felt bad for the woman had his adrenaline not been so high.

"Oh, my God!" Linda exclaimed next to him, whimpering and panting.

"We gotta get to the car, come on," Jack said.

Although the street over here was chaotic too, Jack and Linda weren't in any immediate danger. They went around in hopes of reaching their car, since those three men were blocking it. By the time they reached the car, Jack sighed in relief at luck being on their side.

The men from before were gone, occupied with something they had seen or heard down the street and were now chasing it. Just as Jack opened the door, he saw a figure jumping out of nowhere and tackling Linda on the other side of the car.

"Linda!" he shouted and immediately ran around the car.

Linda was on her back, a raggedy man on top of her, gurgling and snapping his teeth. Linda held him back with her hands, but the man seemed to be too strong. In that moment, Jack didn't think about his own safety. He bull-rushed the man and knocked him off Linda with a fierce cry.

He grabbed him by the neck and swung his fist at his face. The first punch connected with his forehead, causing him to slam his head backward on the pavement. Every subsequent punch came automatically for Jack.

He didn't know what got over him. All he knew was that he wanted to murder this person for trying to hurt Linda. His fist connected with the man's now-limp head over and over. His face was entirely bloody, and Jack only vaguely heard a voice calling to him, as if through a tunnel.

"Jack! We need to go!" Linda tugged him by the shirt, pulling him away from the man.

Only then had Jack seen what he had wrought on the man. His nose was crushed and his face swollen beyond recognition. He would have contemplated whether he had just killed a person if Linda had not reminded him again that they had to go.

They hastily jumped inside the car. Jack immediately locked the doors and reached into his pocket for the car keys.

"Jack?" Linda asked in a small voice in the passenger's seat next to him.

"Yeah, babe?" Jack asked as he pulled out the keys and inserted them into the ignition.

"We need to hurry," Linda said.

She sounded calm when she said that, but Jack could sense the impatience in her tone. He instinctively looked up and saw a group of people, who weren't there just a moment ago, rushing toward the car. Their faces were contorted into something Jack could only describe as hate. He heard their muffled screams as they shoved each other in an attempt to be the first one to reach the newly found prey.

Jack turned the key in the ignition and the car roared to life. He couldn't run the people over. They were people, after all. He stepped on the gas and veered to the right, trying to avoid the group in a wide arc. They readjusted their direction and went after the car. They didn't look like they cared that they were about to be run over.

Jack further jerked the steering wheel right. The car climbed on top of the sidewalk and scratched against the wall, trundling along the way. Even with the car practically kissing the building, the group of people ran in front of it. The car bumped into a young woman at full force while running over a man who had fallen beneath the tire. The car's left side violently bounced, and Jack thought he heard a crack under the tires.

The group of people was now effectively behind the car, but the woman who Jack had bumped into was on top of the hood, her hands and face pressed against the windshield. Linda screamed, and Jack sharply turned left to try to shake the woman off the car.

Her hands and mouth left a trail of red smears on the glass. The strands of her hair stuck together from the blood that crusted it, and her fingernails and clothes were coated in mud. She had a large splotch of red on her chest, and Jack saw chipped front teeth when she opened her mouth to hiss.

There was no humanity in those eyes. Only hunger. The people inside the car were nothing but a meal to her, and the only thing stopping her from eating was the thick pane of glass.

"Get off!" Jack shouted, but he might as well have been talking to a wall.

Zig-zagging only caused the woman to slightly loll left and right, but she remained firmly on the car. By then, they were well out of Eugene on the open road. Jack stepped on the gas pedal as hard as he could, allowing the car to gain speed.

"Linda, put on your seatbelt!" Jack said.

He saw Linda looking at him briefly before complying. The car was reaching seventy miles per hour. It would have to do. As soon as Linda was strapped in, Jack let go of the gas and stepped on the brake pedal as hard as he could. The tires screeched, and both he and Linda lurched forward. The woman on the hood slid off the car, as if she had been vacuumed by something in the air, and flew about fifteen feet before finally landing on the pavement.

There was a sickening crack as she landed, and then, there was silence.

Jack's and Linda's panting filled the car's interior. They were both focused on the woman, who was lying on her side, facing away from them. Jack looked at Linda. Her chest rose and fell violently. Her forehead and neck glistened from the beads of sweat, and her hands trembled as she held the sides of the seat.

"You okay?" Jack asked.

She nodded fervently. Jack swallowed and gently put his foot on the gas pedal. The car started moving forward. He drove around the woman, keeping a close eye on her. Linda craned her neck to see her, as well. When they drove past her, Jack saw an unnatural bulge on the side of the woman's neck. Her eyes stared into empty space. There was no life in them.

"Oh, my God…" Linda exclaimed in a sigh.

"We had no choice. She attacked us," Jack said.

Jack pressed the gas pedal harder, increasing the speed of the car. He put his hand on the back of Linda's neck and gently caressed her with his thumb. He looked in the rearview mirror back at Eugene. The chaos was still visible from here. The smoke that they had seen earlier was now thicker, spreading into the entire sky above the town.

"Babe… your hand…" Linda said with horror on her face.

Jack felt his heart jump into his throat.

Oh, crap. I must have cut myself while punching that man. That means I'm infected.

He looked at his knuckles, scrutinizing them with rigid detail. They were bruised, but there were no scratches or open wounds on them. He breathed a sigh of relief, only just then feeling the pulsating in his hand.

"It's fine," he said breathlessly. "It's fine."

"What is going on here?" Linda asked.

Jack shook his head and moved the rearview mirror up so that he didn't need to look at the mess in the town.

"Whatever it is, we'll be safer on the farm," he said.

Chapter One

The annoying alarm clock blared in the bedroom. Jack jumped into the sitting position. He looked around the room, expecting trouble. Ever since The Collapse, he had become a light sleeper. In fact, he didn't even know why he still set the alarm clock. He was too sleepy for deep contemplation, but he aloofly came to the conclusion that he did it because it was a habit.

And you want to maintain a sense of normalcy.

Jack slammed the top of the alarm clock with the palm of his hand to shut it up. Even after it stopped ringing, his head hurt from the incessant noise. Jack threw the sheets off and got up. The wood flooring felt cold to the touch, a testament to the fact that winter was coming.

As much as Jack liked winter before, he no longer wanted it to arrive out of practical reasons. Surviving on the farm during the cold weather would be much harder now that access to regular supplies and heating was cut off.

Jack sauntered to the window and glanced outside. It was overcast, and it would probably rain again later today. Even from here, he could see the dew that had collected on the grass. Jack ran a hand down his face and then rubbed his eyes. He wanted nothing more than to go back to bed, but he had work to do. He could sleep later.

He donned his clothes and sluggishly stepped out of the bedroom. He glanced to the left down the corridor. No noise came from the adjacent room the entire night, and that worried him. He would need to deal with that a little later.

Jack walked downstairs and then stepped outside on the porch. He pulled out a pack of cigarettes and a lighter. He took one half-smoked cigarette out and put it in his mouth while scanning the wire fence from left to right. There was one straggler in the meadow, a few hundred feet away from the property. Jack squinted at the person.

It was difficult to discern any features on the person from here. It might have been a man with long hair, in a coat. It might have been a woman, too. Jack figured that there was no point in going out there to clear the place of that one infected person. It was always safer waiting for them to come to the fence.

Once his cigarette was lit, Jack made his way to the fence and began his morning round of inspections. He walked alongside the fence and gave it a good rattle every couple of feet to see if it held well. The farm's fence stretched at least three hundred feet on each side, so Jack's inspection was also his early morning physical activity.

The front side of the fence was okay. The gate also still held strong. Jack would sometimes hear the fence rattling at night. At first, he was bothered by it. He would get out of bed, get his revolver, and make sure to clear everything out. That wasn't such a great idea, because he found that there were nights when he couldn't get more than an hour of sleep before being disturbed again by the stragglers. Instead, he learned to ignore it, slept like a baby, and then cleared the fence in the morning if they were still there.

The fence stretching along the right side of the farmstead was okay. On the backside, he found traces of blood. When Jack bent down to inspect it, he saw that the bottom of the fence was slightly damaged. Part of the mesh detached from the rest, and if pushed really hard, a rodent could get inside. The last thing Jack needed was for a fox or something like that to come and kill his remaining chickens. He decided that he would fix the fence a bit later.

He checked the rest of the property until he was full-circle back in front of the house. Everything else was fine. He then went inside the chicken coop located at the back of the farm. The coop itself was constructed to look like a tiny house with a plank placed as a bridge leading down from the door to the ground. The area was fenced off with its own tall mesh fence – something to stop the chickens from escaping since they could hop so high up.

Four chickens were in the yard of the coop, walking around and pecking the ground. Jack peeked inside, but he couldn't tell how many more chickens remained. It had been days since he counted them, and he assumed that no more than eight remained. That was worrisome.

He retrieved a handful of corn from the bag leaning on the back of the house and tossed it inside the coop through the mesh. The corn rained down on the chickens, and immediately, the animals began clucking loudly and speeding around the coop, eager to grab as many pieces of corn into their beaks as they could. Jack threw two more handfuls for them.

When The Collapse first came, he was very sparing with the food he fed the animals, because he didn't know how quickly it would run out. The farm had over twenty chickens back then, and he only had four bags of food for them. Now, he still had almost one full bag of corn and another unopened bag of grains, and he assumed that it would be more than enough to last him until all the chickens were gone.

Leaving the animals to eat, Jack returned into the house and decided that it was time for him to have breakfast, too. He wasn't particularly hungry, but he decided that he should probably eat now so that he didn't need to interrupt his work later.

Since the electricity no longer worked, and he didn't want to use the backup generator for something as insignificant as cooking, he went into the pantry and grabbed a can of baked beans. Jack hated baked beans at first because they smelled and tasted like dog food to him, but he started liking them eventually. In fact, he started liking them so much that he ate them even when it wasn't on the agenda.

Jack would have loved to have some coffee to go with that, but he was all out. Instead, he took a bottle of water from the fridge and drank a few sips after breakfast. He then went to do his inventory. He should have done that days ago, but lately, he'd been feeling really tired. He slept enough, but he still felt tired for some reason.

There were a number of things that Jack needed to keep a track of, so he had it all in his notebook on the coffee table in the living room. He grabbed the notebook and the pen and went to count the ammo in the wardrobe first. Still forty-two rounds remaining. He also inspected the handgun. It had been a while since he used it, and he chided himself for not cleaning it already. The last thing he wanted was a jammed gun during an emergency.

Just like the fence, he would do that later.

Jack closed the wardrobe and looked at the notes. Next to "Ammo", the last number in the series of digits was forty-two, so he didn't change anything. He then went into the pantry to count the food. That was something that dwindled fast. Despite that, the pantry was still filled with an abundance of processed meat cans, tuna cans, baked beans, military MREs, and so on.

There were some disgusting foods in there that Jack decided he would touch only when he had nothing else left to eat. For example, canned hamburger looked soggy and disgusting even on the label – it resembled something you'd leave out on the porch for a few days – and Jack knew that once he opened that can, the burger would be even less appetizing.

There were other foods that he really wanted to try, but was saving them for emergencies, like chocolate bars, crackers, mac n' cheese. He figured he'd eat one of those later today, why not?

For now, he closed the pantry and put the number in the notebook, trying not to cringe at how much smaller it had gotten. He then went outside to count the chickens. His previous estimation was close. Only nine chickens remained. He grabbed the three eggs they laid and went back inside the house. The straggler from before was now close to the woods, still aimlessly pacing around.

Jack went inside and put the eggs inside the egg carton on the windowsill – the fridge no longer worked, of course, so he no longer kept the food there. He went into the living room and slumped into the sofa facing the TV. On the black screen, he saw his own distended reflection. Sometimes in the quiet moments, he'd stare at that reflection and imagine that another person was inside the TV, having his own world and living his own farm life identical to Jack's. Sometimes, it became unnerving to think that way.

The wall clock ticked with each passing second, intermittently breaking the silence in the room. Jack looked at it. It was nine fifty-four AM. The book that Jack had started reading weeks ago was on the coffee table. It hadn't been touched in days, and he wanted to go back to reading it – especially since he had nothing better to do during the majority of the day – but he has just been so lazy.

The clock's ticking worked hypnotically like a metronome, and Jack felt his eyelids becoming heavy. He forcibly blinked. He didn't want to sleep, but it was so difficult for him to keep his eyes open. He allowed them to close, telling himself that he would rest his eyes for just a moment.

Before he knew it, he had already started falling asleep.

Chapter Two

The laughter that came from her was contagious. It was laughter that he wanted to hear again, over and over, for the rest of his life.

Jack had been having trouble with his internet service provider for a while now. He had tried canceling the plan, but then they had informed him that he would need to pay a cancelation fee. He was also told that the cancelation request needs two to three weeks to get processed, and he would need to fully pay for that time if it went into the next month.

When Jack's cancelation for the plan finally got approved, he was informed that he needed to arrive to the provider on a specific date in order to finalize the cancelation. When he arrived, they told him that the date he was given was wrong, and he would now need to pay for the following month and request a new cancelation.

By then, Jack was fed up with those goddamn service providers and he demanded that something be done about it immediately. He felt bad for yelling at the young woman wearing the name tag "Penelope" because she was only doing her job, but he had lost his patience. The heads of all the staff and customers in the room had turned to face Jack.

After five or so minutes of going back and forth and not reaching a consensus, another employee stepped in to rectify the situation. She was young, maybe in her mid-twenties and very cute. The way she smiled at Jack immediately defused him. It wasn't a taut rictus that employees usually flashed their clients in a patronizing manner. No, this looked like a genuine smile. Not only did it calm Jack down, but it made him feel embarrassed for reacting the way he did.

"Hi, sir. I would like to help you with your problem. Would you mind coming with me?" she asked politely.

Her voice was a melody to Jack's ears. He nodded and followed the girl to her window, just then realizing how quiet the room had fallen. Gradually, the voices resumed, forgetting all about Jack's outburst. Jack slightly leaned over the counter, partly in order to hear the girl better over the murmuring of the other customers, but mostly because he felt a strong desire to get closer to her.

"So, would you mind telling me what the problem is, sir?" she asked.

"Jack. Call me Jack," he said. He then looked at the girl's name tag. It said "Linda." "Well, Linda, here's my problem."

He proceeded to explain everything. Linda listened attentively the entire time, nodding and uttering phrases like "hmm" and "okay". The entire time, Jack felt like he was being listened to, especially because Linda mentioned how she had similar troubles in the past. Jack wasn't sure if it was her specific way of dealing with difficult customers, or if she was just making natural small talk with him – he hoped for the latter.

She looked something up in the system, and Jack used that moment to shamelessly stare at her. She wasn't wearing a lot of makeup, Jack noticed from the screen's brightness that illuminated her face. She had freckles on her nose, and he found them attractive.

He knew that some women would go above and beyond to hide any blemishes on their face with makeup, and while Jack didn't have anything against them doing that, he found the flaws that everyone had on their faces only made them look special and more attractive.

Linda briefly darted her eyes from the screen to Jack, and then quickly looked back at the monitor. Jack looked away as well, embarrassed that she caught him staring. He cleared his throat and pretended to be occupied with something on the counter.

"The system is a little slow, so just bear with me a little longer, Jack," Linda said.

The slower the better, Jack wanted to say aloud. After a few minutes of Linda clicking on the mouse, she turned to Jack and started explaining what his options were. He was only half-listening. He was so mesmerized by her eyes that he could hardly pay attention to what she was saying.

When Linda finished explaining, Jack continued nodding. Only a few seconds of senseless nodding later did he realize that Linda had in fact finished speaking.

"So, uh…" He scratched his cheek. "You're the pro. What do you suggest I do?"

Linda flashed him that same enchanting smile again. She proceeded to explain what she would do if it were her, and again, Jack tried to focus really hard, but the technical mumbo-jumbo, coupled with the fact that he was nervous as heck in front of this cutie, made it really difficult for him to catch everything she was saying.

Once again, he was caught off guard when she finished speaking. He nervously cleared his throat and shrugged. "Okay, um… sure. Let's do that," he said and hoped that she wasn't asking him a question.

Linda's mouth morphed into a half-smile as she turned toward the screen. Jack wasn't sure what the smile indicated. Maybe she found it funny that he was so clumsy. He suddenly felt like a moron. A hundred thoughts like those raced through his mind while Linda typed something on the computer.

A minute or so later, she gave him a paper to sign. He took the pen and gave her a suspicious glance. "Not selling my soul to you, am I?" he asked, and just then realized how stupid the joke sounded.

Whether it was genuine or out of courtesy, Linda laughed. It was a contagious laughter. It was laughter that Jack wanted to hear again. He signed the paper and Linda gave him his copy of whatever that thing was.

"There you go, all set, Jack," she said amicably and leaned on the counter.

They were only inches away from each other now. He smelled something fruity on her. Strawberry, maybe? Jack was bad at identifying smells. Either way, the pleasant smell on Linda was just barely discernible.

"Let me just see what I signed here, if you don't mind," Jack said and pressed harder against the counter, inching closer to Linda.

"Take all the time you need," Linda said.

Jack pretended to read through the contract, nodding and occasionally looking at Linda to ask her what this or that meant. She explained everything with clarity and brevity – not like the other employees who sounded like they spoke in a different language when they talked about packages.

When Jack finally reached the end of the paper, he scratched his cheek. His brain was screaming at him to do what he had in mind, but another part of him told him that it was crazy. Before he could chicken out, he said, "I see only one problem with this."

"Okay, and what's that?" Linda asked with confusion on her face.

By then, Jack's heart was drumming in his chest like crazy. "I don't see your number written anywhere on it," he said as he slid the paper to Linda.

He tried not to break eye contact as he said so, in order to give Linda the illusion of being confident. Linda looked down at the paper, and then up at Jack. *What were you thinking, you creep? She's going to ask you to leave now.*

But then, Linda flashed him a tight-lipped smile. She looked like she was trying to maintain a reserved stare. She took the pen and clicked it on while maintaining eye contact with Jack.

And then she wrote her number.

Chapter Three

Jack opened his eyes to the sound of scratching coming from upstairs. For a moment, he was lost in time and space. He glanced at the wall clock. Three minutes past ten AM. He must have dozed off, and it felt like he had slept for hours, rather than minutes.

He forcibly blinked three times to wake up, but couldn't get up from the sofa. His body felt like it weighed a hundred tons more than it should, and he needed another moment to collect himself. His eyelids were still droopy. Jack rested his head on the backrest of the sofa and closed his eyes again.

The scratching from upstairs came again, low, but just loud enough for Jack to hear it. Jack instinctively looked at the ceiling. The scratching came unpredictably at different intervals, sometimes taking longer pauses in between, sometimes shorter, sometimes the scratching sounded like something was dragged alongside the entire length of the floor, sometimes short and mouse-like, focused on one tiny spot.

But one thing was consistent – it was there.

The harder Jack tried to ignore it, the more it persisted. It became so loud now that he felt like the grating was coming from right inside his ears. Back when Jack lived with his parents in Oregon City, they had a mice infestation in the attic, so hearing the scratching at night was something Jack was accustomed to.

It even worked as a background noise that helped him fall asleep more easily. He never once caught any mice in the home when living there, and his parents were the types of people who wouldn't bother to take care of something unless it really caused an inconvenience or a lot of damage.

The last time he went to visit his parents with Linda, the scratching was still there. They were supposed to sleep over in Jack's old room, but the problem was that the attic was just above, and the epicenter of the scratching was the loudest there.

When Jack and Linda first went to bed and she heard the scratching, she grabbed Jack by the wrist and froze. Even in the darkness, he could see her staring at him with a wide-eyed look of fear.

"What is that?" she asked.

"Oh, just the mice," Jack said.

"Mice?!" Linda asked.

Jack jumped to explain that it's not dangerous like she thought it was, but Linda had already grabbed her phone and turned on the torch. She shone it all around the floor, the walls, and then held it pointed at the ceiling. Even when Jack tried calming her down so that they could fall asleep, Linda was perturbed.

"What if they gnaw through the wall and fall on us?" she asked.

"Babe, I've lived here for years, and the scratching has been here for a while. I've never seen a mouse in this house," Jack said.

"Okay," Linda said, but Jack could hear the uncertainty in her voice.

She turned off the torch and tried to fall asleep, but whenever the scratching became louder, she turned it back on and pointed it at the ceiling, just to make sure a hole hadn't appeared in there while she wasn't looking. She then searched stuff online about mice and how dangerous they can be. Jack told her not to do it, because search engines always gave the worst-case scenario information. Sure enough, looking up things about mice online didn't calm Linda down. Eventually, Jack suggested they both sleep downstairs on the couch.

That worked better for the both of them. There were no scratching noises, and they had to sleep hugged tightly against each other because the couch was small. Jack often remembered that night with relish. He knew that Linda was scared of mice, but there was something about her that made him fall in love with her even more when she wasn't afraid to cling to him when she got scared.

The scratching upstairs now sounded faster and more impatient. Jack rubbed his eyes and forced himself to stand up with a huff. He sauntered toward the front door and stepped outside. Light drizzle had started, its soft pitter-patter permeating the air. It was much colder all of a sudden, too. It immediately helped Jack shake off the remainder of grogginess that lingered on him.

He walked around the house toward the chicken coop. Five chickens were outside, already drenched from the rain, but seemed not to mind. They clucked, walked around, jerked their heads in random directions, not paying attention to Jack. Jack reached down into the coop to grab the closest chicken.

As if sensing what was coming, the chicken fluttered its wings and moved away from Jack with a loud cluck. Jack cursed under his breath and opened the tiny gate of the coop. He stepped inside and closed the gate, watching the chickens disperse at his presence.

He grabbed the calmest-looking one who stood in the corner and put it under his arm. The chicken didn't resist, but just to be on the safe side, Jack pressed it against his side in a way that it couldn't flail its wings.

Jack exited the coop and walked back into the house. The drizzle had started to turn into full-blown rain by then. When Jack entered the house and closed the door, the pattering on the roof intensified. He liked listening to that sound when he had no work to do. It calmed him down and made him want to sleep.

His face was covered in rain, so he wiped it with his sleeve. He walked upstairs, where the battering of the rain only became louder. The scratching was either gone, or was so low that he couldn't hear it. He walked to the end of the corridor and approached the last door on the left.

The first thing Jack did was lean his ear against the door to listen for any sounds. It was quiet. Jack knocked on the door with his free hand. No response came. He fished a key out of his pocket – he always kept that key on him – and inserted it into the keyhole. He turned the key twice, listening to the loud clicking of the lock.

He then waited again. Still no sounds. Slowly, Jack opened the door and peeked inside. The room smelled horrible. It somewhat resembled the smell of the chicken coop's interior, but much worse. He really wished that he could reach the window to open it for some fresh air.

The room had a bed in the corner. The mattress was stained with patinas of dust and crusted blood. The floor was littered with tiny bones, feathers, and rotting meat. In front of the window stood a figure, facing outside. Her hair was disheveled, the strands messily jutting in various directions. The woman's blouse had a bevy of sickly colors on them, including red, brown, and in some patches, the original blue that it once was. Her jeans were torn in places, and Jack saw bloodied scratches there.

The woman stood perfectly still, her head slightly tilted, her arms lamely hanging on her sides. Soft wheezing sounds came out in slow and steady breaths, as if she was trying to breathe through a straw.

"Hi, Linda," Jack said. "I brought you breakfast, baby."

He pushed the door open widely. It creaked, drowning out the pattering sounds on the roof for a brief moment. Jack took a step inside.

"I know I don't have a lot of variety to give you, but you refuse to eat anything else, so here–"

Linda spun around and ran toward Jack with her hands outstretched in front of her. Jack didn't even have time to react. But just as she got an inch away from him, she stopped. The chain that went from the link in the floor to Linda's waist rattled and became taut under her effort to reach Jack.

She growled and hissed, desperately trying to reach Jack. Her fingers clawed at the air, so close to Jack's face that he could see the broken, dirty fingernails and the fingers covered in dried blood. Her wedding ring was crusted with brown stains. Jack took a moment to look at Linda's face.

Her face was dirty. A wet strand of hair fell over her face. She had a small diagonal scar on her forehead that had been there for days now. It was worse than a few days ago, when Jack first thought that it would heal. There was pus in the wound, and the red line had morphed to black instead.

Linda's mouth was open, and spittle flew out as she violently growled and gnashed her teeth. Hot putrid breath hit Jack in the face, almost causing him to gag.

Blood smeared the corners of her lips. Linda's once hazel eyes had turned pallid, as if she had gone blind, but Jack knew for a fact that she saw him, because whenever he was in the room, her eyes were always fixated on him.

"Babe, come on. Please, don't be like this," Jack said. Tears welled up in his eyes at the sight of Linda behaving the way she did. "I can't remove the chains until you stop attacking me. I know you're still in there. I know you remember me. You just need to fight that urge to eat me."

Jack grabbed the chicken with both hands. He felt the chicken trying to resist with its wings, but Jack held it firmly. Linda's fingers still clawed at the air, rattling the chain violently. She was fighting so hard against her restrains that Jack figured she must have badly abraded her skin around the waist. He would need to remove the chain for a few days to give her a break.

"Here you go, babe," Jack said and tossed the chicken into the corner of the room behind Linda.

The chicken fluttered its wings before landing. As soon as Jack tossed the animal, Linda turned her head in a jerky motion toward it. She fell on top of the chicken before the poor animal could even understand what was going on.

Linda grabbed the chicken and sunk her teeth into it. The chicken clucked more violently as blood spurted out of it. Linda took bite after bite, feathers and meat sticking out of her mouth. The chicken's spasmodic movement waned very soon, and then it stopped moving and clucking altogether while Linda continued eating it. The room was filled with loud crunching and squelching sounds, along with Linda's shallow, wheezy breaths between each bite.

"I have to get back to work, sweetie. I'll come visit you tonight again, alright?" Jack said.

Linda gave no indication that she heard Jack at all. Jack felt an irresistible urge to approach her and kiss her on the head. He took a step closer to her. He was now within her chain range. He bent down and reached toward the back of her head with his fingers. He hadn't even realized how much they trembled. His fingers inched closer to Linda's head.

Gently, the tips of his fingers brushed her hair. It felt cold and wet to the touch. She still didn't acknowledge his presence. Her face was now messily buried in the chicken's stomach as she chewed its insides, getting blood all over her face.

Jack became more confident with the lack of Linda's response, and he caressed her head. It felt like caressing seaweed and hay. He would give Linda a bath these days, as soon as he figured out how to do it. He also needed to give her a fresh change of clothes.

"I love you, Linda," Jack said.

Linda's response was biting the head of the chicken. Jack walked out of the room, took one final glance at Linda, and then closed the door and locked it.

Chapter Four

Even in the most difficult moments, she didn't need to do anything. As soon as she flashed him that enchanting smile that made him fall in love with her, he knew that everything was going to be okay because he had her by his side.

Jack texted Linda the same day when he got her number. She hadn't responded until later that night. She apologized and told him that she just recently finished her shift. Jack asked her more about her job, and she told him that she'd been working there for a few years now, but studied to get a master's degree in botany.

That impressed Jack beyond words. Moreover, it made him feel like an underachiever compared to Linda. That's why he didn't know how to answer when she asked him about his work. Jack worked at Eugene's local antique shop, and it was pretty much as boring and underwhelming as it sounded, so he hoped that Linda wouldn't be put off by it.

If anything, she seemed intrigued by his job. Jack told her that he preferred talking about it in person when they went on a date. It was another risky move on his end, but it paid off, because Linda agreed almost immediately.

Jack didn't want to go to a restaurant where they would be forced to talk to each other and potentially create awkward silence. Instead, he asked Linda if she wanted to go rafting on the Willamette River. Linda said that she never went rafting, but she always wanted to try it. Jack assured her that he would show her all the ropes.

They agreed to go out in two days. Jack wanted to be a gentleman, so he offered to pick Linda up, but she didn't want him to go through the hassle and said they could meet there. They continued texting that same night until around two AM, and they texted the following, which made Jack regret that he didn't set the date up for a day sooner. They talked about the stuff they did in their free time, their families, their plans for the future, and similar.

When the day of the date finally came, Jack was nervous as hell. He spent two hours preparing himself for it. He hadn't gone out on a date in well over six months after breaking up with Eugenia because he needed the time to recuperate, and he wasn't sure how to prepare for a rafting date since he had never been on one.

Linda looked exactly the same way she did when the two of them first met, and yet somehow, she was more beautiful. Jack felt the temperature rising when he saw her, even though it was still early spring. His brain suddenly malfunctioned. Should he go for a hug? A handshake? Just say hi?

Luckily, Linda took the initiative. She took a step forward and gave Jack a light hug. They rented the raft from the crotchety old man working at the dock, and he explained what they can and can't do. He warned them to take the left turn, and under no circumstances to go right because the current was more turbulent there. He also warned them not to scratch the raft or they would need to pay for it. Jack paid the man without grumbling and he and Linda put on the helmets and the life vests before getting into the raft.

Since there were only two of them, the raft was smaller, and they could face each other, which worked in Jack's favor. They paddled away from the shore and let the current of the river take them. It was relatively calm, and the raft's trundling was miniscule. Linda had a smile on her face as she glanced around the Douglas firs that stretched on either side of the river.

"Wow, it's so peaceful," she said.

"I figured you'd like it. You're a botanist, so you must like nature, right?" Jack asked.

Linda glanced at him and her smile stretched further. She was visibly flattered that Jack decided to take her to a place that he thought she would appreciate. She leaned to the side and allowed her fingers to skim the surface of the water. A moment later, she retracted her hand with a gasp.

"Something just touched me," she said. "Something… pink."

"Rainbow trout," Jack said. "There's a whole lot of them in the river. Don't worry, they're harmless. You're at more danger of dying from hypothermia than the fish in these waters."

Linda looked at him, intrigue forming on her face. "How do you know that?" she asked.

Jack shrugged. "I'm no botanist, or scientist, or anything *ist*, but I know a lot about animals. I'm building my own house in the countryside and I plan to live there in the future and have some animals."

Jack didn't want to use the word "farm" because he thought it would make him sound like a hillbilly.

"I always wanted to live in the countryside," Linda said. "My grandpa left me his property just outside Springfield a few years ago, but I didn't know any better and I sold it. I still regret making that mistake."

"Never too late to start a life in the countryside." Jack's mouth contorted into a grin. He could suddenly imagine his life with Linda on the farm. He would be tending to the animals, and she would collect the plants that they could use for… whatever plants were used for.

She glanced around, smiling, and admiring the beauty that surrounded the raft, but Jack was focused on her, admiring the beauty inside the raft. That moment was short-lived, because when she looked at him, her eyes widened, and she opened her mouth to warn Jack about something behind him.

An icy wave splashed the raft, instantly snapping Jack out of his daydreaming stupor. The wave enveloped Linda for a moment, the water foaming around the raft. Jack immediately grabbed the oars. The raft bobbed up and down and left and right, and Jack had to hold on really tight in order to not fall out of the raft.

Linda screamed and jerked to the side, but Jack grabbed her by the arm to keep her inside. More cold waves splashed the raft, causing Jack's already cold fingers to become numb. While staring at Linda, he completely forgot to take the turn that the old man warned them about.

The raft now moved so fast that Jack expected to capsize if they ran into the smallest obstacle. He looked down the river and saw that it stretched pretty far before veering to the right, which would further take them off course. The crashing and lapping of the waves were so loud now that Jack had to yell for Linda to hear him.

He told her to help him paddle toward the shore, and she nodded. By the time they got relatively close to the shore, they could no longer reach it, because the ground was elevated and they had no way of climbing up from the raft. All they could do was hope that the current wouldn't take them too far. Jack had no idea where the river ended, only that it led northward. Worst-case scenario, they would end up in Portland.

Their luck changed when the river swerved to the right and their raft was taken all the way to the other side of the shore. The raft landed on the sandy ground with a loud scratching sound before reaching a complete halt. Jack looked at Linda, who was holding onto the oars for dear life. The booming sounds of the water around them were now in the background, still loud, but much less so.

"Linda! Are you okay?" Jack asked, shivering from the cold and feeling like a complete moron.

Linda looked around the raft, as if to make sure the ride was really over. It must have been at least twenty minutes since they left the dock where they started. She looked at him and snorted. It took Jack a moment to understand that she was laughing. She laughed really hard, and that made Jack laugh with her. He wasn't sure if they were laughing out of relief, or because it was funny now that they looked back.

When they were done laughing, Jack stepped out of the raft, and Linda mimicked his gesture. He approached the shore and looked left and then right. One thing was for sure. There was no way that they'd be able to go back the way they came with the raft. They were supposed to take the left turn, and then leave the raft at the checkpoint, where they could rent a quad to go back toward Eugene. Now, they were stranded in the middle of the woods.

"Okay, so um… I guess we're going hiking. If that's okay with you," Jack said.

"What about the raft?" Linda asked.

Jack looked at the raft. There was no way he'd be able to carry it. "Well, I'll tell the old man where it is and hope he doesn't get too angry."

"We can split the bill if we have to pay for it," Linda said.

Jack suppressed the warm feeling forming inside him. "No way," he said. "This was my bad, so I'll take full responsibility."

They began walking through the woods. There was no trail, so they went alongside the river. For the first two minutes, they didn't talk. But then Linda pointed somewhere and took a short detour. She stopped in front of a violet corn-shaped plant growing from the ground and turned to Jack.

"Do you know what this is?" she asked.

"I do not," Jack said. "Looks pretty, though." He reached for it, but then Linda slapped him on the wrist.

"That's *Digitalis Purpurea*, or foxglove," Linda said.

"Is it an endangered plant or something?"

"No. It's highly poisonous. It's used for heart medication, but it's also a deadly poison. Back when I was in college, they wouldn't let us even get close to the plant when demonstrating how to take extracts."

"Wow. So, if I ever get on your bad side, you can kill me with poison."

Linda smiled at him and continued walking. "Or I can heal you if you ever get badly injured."

Jack contemplated cracking a joke about being injured right now, but once again, he waited because he wasn't sure if Linda would appreciate his sense of humor when they've only known each other for such a short time.

As they walked, every now and again, Linda would stop to point to a certain plant. Jack would ask her about the plants in detail. He found the information interesting, and he could tell why someone would choose to be a botanist. Linda assured him that she was only sharing the fun things, and that over ninety-five percent of botany studying revolved around the boring theoretical stuff and Latin words.

Still, Linda talked about botany with passion. She said that she loved planting a seed and then seeing it grow into something strong thanks to her nurturing. Jack loved listening to her talk. Linda could talk about astrophysics and mathematical formulae and Jack would still be mesmerized by her voice.

After walking for some time, they reached the confluence where they should have taken the left turn. The problem was, they were stuck between the forked rivers, and needed to backtrack on the other side in hopes of finding a bridge or some place where they could walk across.

The sky had already turned orange by then, and Linda complained about freezing. Jack suggested they take a break, while he went to gather some sticks. She asked him what he was doing, but he told her to wait and see. He didn't have a lighter or anything that would help him, but he knew how to start a fire with a spindle. Sometimes, it took him a little longer to do it, but he figured that this was a great way to impress Linda.

Or to look like a moron, a doubtful voice in his head said.

"You're going to start a fire?" Linda asked.

"Uh-huh." Jack nodded as he spun the spindle between his palms, causing friction at the tip.

The piece of wood at the bottom was already starting to produce smoke, and it wouldn't be long until the ember formed. Jack was focused on the spindle, constantly moving his palms back up toward the top of the spindle in order to maintain the continuous friction.

When the ember finally formed, he took the spindle out and blew into the source of the smoke before transferring the glowing ember into the clump of tree bark that he had collected on a pile earlier. The bark ignited, and Jack blew further into it until the fire finally appeared.

Linda clapped in excitement. Jack placed the bark down and added tiny pieces of twigs to nurture the flame. From there, it was easy creating a campfire. Linda's jaw hung to the floor. She didn't even need to say anything for Jack to see how impressed she was.

They sat next to each other in front of the fire. Linda was shivering and Jack wanted nothing more than to hug her to keep her warm. The warmth and the crackling of the wood were soothing, but Jack felt like he could be just a little warmer – if only he sat a little closer to Linda. Linda held her palms toward the fire, warming herself up. She thanked Jack for making the fire, and he reminded her that it was his fault they were in this mess in the first place.

Suddenly, Linda stood up and left, telling Jack that she'd be back in a few minutes. Sure enough, she returned some time later with grape-like berries in her hands. "Try it," she said.

"Are you trying to poison me?" Jack joked.

Linda ate one grape in front of him to show him that it was safe. Jack shrugged and took one as well. They tasted nothing like grapes, but they did have a sweet tinge to them. Linda proceeded to tell Jack about the plant and how it's used not just as an edible berry, but also for medicinal purposes.

"Well, we'd make a great team, huh?" Jack asked. "I could start fires and make shelters for us, and you could fetch us edible berries and treat our wounds."

"Who knows, maybe on that farm of yours one day we might even do that." Linda winked. Jack's ears started burning pleasantly when she said that.

They were sitting really close to each other, their faces mere inches apart. They gazed at each other for a moment, their eyes locked in a staring contest. Her hair was wet, and she looked beautiful. Jack had an uncontrollable urge to lean in and kiss her, like a powerful magnet that he couldn't pull away from. It was so strong that he suddenly felt out of breath. His heart pumped faster than it did in the raft.

He gave into the urge and leaned toward Linda. She did the same. Their lips lightly brushed at first, and then locked. Jack felt a shockwave of something pleasant surging through his entire body. He explored Linda's lips, softly and probingly.

She put a hand on his cheek. That encouraged him to pull her closer to him. Their bodies were now pressed tightly together, and he felt like it still wasn't close enough to her. Minutes might have gone by, but to Jack, that felt like mere seconds. He wanted to freeze the moment, but luck would not have it.

A voice called out to them, interrupting their moment of passion. The ranger who had found them asked what was going on, and soon, they were safely escorted out of the woods. Jack got into an argument with the old man, and he ended up paying him a small fee for the damages, but all of that faded into nothingness compared to the electric kiss he and Linda shared again later when he walked her home.

As he watched her leave, Jack couldn't imagine that only five months later they would indeed be living together in the countryside, doing exactly what they talked about at the campfire.

Chapter Five

The munching sounds in Linda's room stopped not long after Jack exited. He hadn't even realized that he was holding his breath until he turned the key and locked the door once again. He suddenly felt even more drained than he was when he fell asleep on the couch.

Visiting Linda in her room was becoming harder and harder for him. It was difficult to see her deteriorating to the state she was in. What would happen in the end? Would her body continue decomposing until there was nothing but rot and bone remaining? Would she continue to display the same hunger even then?

Back when radio and TV channels still worked, Jack attentively listened to what the government was instructing – before they disappeared, too. There was a frequency on the radio that always talked about the infection itself. It was a small outpost set up inside Eugene's cathedral by a group of people.

They didn't have any laboratories to investigate what was going on, of course, and back then the government had been too busy trying not to let the wave of the undead spread to the capitals. The person on the radio – he said his name was Gary – talked about the infection, speculating how it had started, what had happened, and so on.

We can see that the people display rabies-like symptoms very quickly. If you get bitten, you'll start to feel itchy all over your body. You'll want to scratch yourself, but the scratch is deep inside all your nerves, and it might even drive you crazy enough to use something sharp to get to that itch. You'll become way more irritable, and everything will make you angry. You'll be very hungry, too. You won't have your cognitive functions anymore by then. You'll only go around, mindlessly attacking and eating the people who you love, no longer in control of yourself. You'll probably know that it's wrong, but the urge is too strong for you to resist.

But this virus, or bacteria, or whatever it is... it doesn't keep the host alive for too long. If you aren't already dead from the bite, then you will be from the infection in a few days. And then... you'll rise again. You will no longer be angry. You will no longer be irritated. You will feel only one thing. The longing for a living person's flesh.

Gary had a soothing voice, and had he been talking about something else, Jack would have easily fallen asleep. He reminded Jack of the narrations on those animal programs that used to run on TV. But Gary never answered one question that's been plaguing Jack's thoughts ever since this whole thing started.

Was the person who resurrected as an undead still with them? Jack firmly believed that Linda was in there, trapped, and no longer in control of herself, but he knew that she was in there. He could see it from the way she sometimes looked at him. He knew that there wasn't just hunger for his flesh in those eyes. He saw it in the miniscule moments when she'd react to certain objects that he showed her – like jerking her head toward her favorite mug, becoming calm when Jack hummed to her, and so on.

She was still here and he didn't care if he had to take care of her for the rest of his life like this. She was the love of his life, and he wasn't going to let anything get in their way.

****

Jack went into the bedroom. He had a radio on the desk over there. He cycled through the frequencies every day for at least two hours – one hour in the morning and one hour in the evening – trying to find whoever was still out there and alive. It had been weeks since he found any working frequency. Even Gary hadn't been broadcasting for a while, much to Jack's disappointment.

Even though he never spoke to Gary, Jack felt like the two of them had formed some kind of alliance during these difficult times. Gary always broadcasted at the same time in the evenings, and those thirty minutes of listening to him helped Jack relax a little and maintain a semblance of normalcy. He wondered what had happened to him.

For a while, the government gave instructions to the people and told them that evacuation would be on the way. That changed when the infection rates surged and the undead could no longer be kept at bay. The military began shooting anyone who had so much as a scratch on them in order to prevent the spread.

Then they decided to bomb all the bridges in Portland in order to stop their advance. Then they talked about nuking the entire city to eliminate the epicenter of the virus. And then they went entirely silent.

Cut off from the rest of the world and in the dark, Jack felt vulnerable for the first few days. He kind of felt like the time when he broke his mobile phone and had to go without it for a few days until he repaired it. But just like with the electricity and the warm water, Jack got used to it.

Getting used to that was the easy part, Jack thought to himself forlornly.

He sat at the desk and stared at the photo of him and Linda plastered to the wall. It was a picture they took together when visiting Santa Barbara. She looked happy in that photo. They both did.

Jack averted his gaze from the picture and began cycling through the radio channels.

****

After an hour of listening to static, Jack leaned back in the chair, resolved to give up. He put his hands behind his head and groaned. Then he slumped his arms back down on the desk. His eyes fell on his wristwatch. It showed three twenty-four. The watch had stopped working months ago, but Jack refused to take it off. It wasn't there for the functionality, but because it was a gift.

He stood up, leaving the radio on Gary's channel in case he decided to make a comeback, and strode out of the room. The rest of the day went by slowly. Jack read about one hundred pages of the book that he had started. He wasn't a fast reader, and that was okay, because the house didn't have a lot of books, so he wanted to stretch them out as much as he could.

He then got a great idea. He decided that he would read to Linda after dinner tonight. After weeks of not doing anything except the daily chores, he suddenly got a little excited about this. He reminded himself that it might be a disappointment – especially if Linda wasn't responsive – but he didn't care. This was not just for her. It was also for him.

****

After eating a can of meat and some leftover homemade bread, Jack had tried making a few days ago, he retrieved another chicken from the coop and fed it to Linda. Whenever he went to the coop and saw the dwindling number of the fowl, he got painfully reminded that in a few days he would have nothing left to feed Linda. She didn't need the canned goods for some reason, only living stuff.

He wanted to reduce her meals to one chicken a day, but the problem was, she ate them up so voraciously – leaving only a few bones and feathers – that he couldn't help but think that she was constantly really hungry. But then again, maybe she was eating them like that because the undead constantly felt the nagging hunger, just like Gary said.

I'll think about it tomorrow. I can't deal with that right now.

He gave Linda some time to enjoy her meal, and then he went to the shelf to pick out a book. There was one called *The Witch of the Woods* that Linda had read aloud in bed almost every night ever since The Collapse had started. The story was short, but she ended up reading it multiple times because she really liked it. Her soothing story-reading voice always put Jack to sleep, even though he always fought to stay awake and listen to her longer.

He took out the book, lit a candle, and went upstairs into Linda's room. The chicken was already gone, more feathers and dried blood added to the already messy room. Linda stood facing Jack, her entire upper body slightly tilted to the side. Her eyes were fixated on him. The disgusting deathly smell was even stronger now, but Jack ignored it.

"Hey, babe," he said. "I thought we could do something interesting tonight." He looked around the room for a spot to sit, but since the floor was so messy, he raised a finger to indicate to Linda to wait. He went downstairs into the kitchen and dragged one chair all the way up to Linda's room. He placed it by the wall next to the door and sat, smiling complacently.

"Recognize this book?" he asked, showing her the front of the cover.

An illustration of a boy and a girl holding hands and walking through the woods was depicted on the cover, with a pair of enormous yellow eyes staring at them from the darkness. Linda stared at Jack, but she gave no indication that she understood what he said.

"You used to read this before bedtime all the time," Jack said. He looked down at the book, suddenly feeling a little melancholic. How he wished he could hear her say something again. Just one word. Anything other than the hissing, wheezing, growling, moaning, and other incoherent sounds.

Linda's throat slightly gurgled. Jack looked at her and smiled. "Sorry, honey. Was just thinking about something. Don't mind me." He opened the book on the first page and cleared his throat. "I can't remember where we stopped. How about we read from the beginning?"

Linda continued staring. Jack looked at the book. The first page showed an illustration of a boy and a girl holding hands and running in a green field under the sun.

"This is my first time narrating something, so go easy on me, okay?" Jack asked. "There once was a boy named Will and a girl named Zara…"

Chapter Six

"Son of a fucking bitch!" Jack exclaimed when he stepped out on the porch.

It was early morning, but he could already tell that he'd have a lot of work today. At least ten infected – or undead, Jack couldn't tell – walked on the meadow beyond the property. They were all thinly spread, each pacing their own way, some of them all the way near the edge of the woods. Jack hadn't cleared the undead off the fence since… well, since Linda turned.

The three closest to the farm turned their heads to face Jack, and as soon as they saw him, they went from lethargically dragging their feet, to growling and dashing toward him. Jack stood still, watching them as they swung their limbs and closed distance between them and Jack. Two of the closest ones were infected, Jack realized, and the one lagging behind was undead. They slammed into the fence, causing the mesh to rattle violently, but doing nothing to compromise the sturdiness of it.

They strained against the wire and tried to reach Jack despite not having any chance of doing so. That was the thing with the infected and the undead. They weren't smart enough to look for an easier way around to reach their victim. They went straight toward the person they chased, whether the path was clear or obstructed.

The last time Jack went to Eugene for a supply run, he saw the undead walking into barbed wire barricades and getting their flesh ripped, and not caring about it one bit. He saw one falling off the second floor and breaking both legs, and still crawling toward Jack. He saw one with a missing arm and guts hanging from its stomach and dragging on the floor, practically tripping it.

All of that made Jack's job a lot easier, but that didn't mean that he liked doing it. He lit up a cigarette and grabbed the pitchfork resting on the porch. The tines still had crusted blood on them from a week ago. Jack hadn't bothered cleaning it, since it only served one purpose.

He sauntered toward the fence, the hungering undead only becoming more violent. Two of them were men in their thirties, and one was a young woman, no older than Linda. The men's faces and clothes were dirty and they had dried bite wounds on their necks. There was no blood around their mouths, which meant that they hadn't taken a bite out of anyone – yet.

Jack couldn't help but wonder how they had managed to survive as an infected for that long if they hadn't eaten. There was a clear difference between the infected and the undead. The infected were still alive and needed their bodily functions to survive. The undead were the infected who had died and then came back to life. No one knew how it worked – all they knew was that the undead were slower and could function as long as their head was uninjured.

Jack approached the fence until he was inches away from the zombies. The man in front of him pressed his face against the fence so hard that he drew blood from his lips and cheek. The fence rattled violently as he snapped his teeth at the air. Jack raised the pitchfork and thrust it forward. The tine pierced the man through the eye with a squelching sound, instantly causing him to stop straining against the fence. Jack pulled the pitchfork out, and the man slumped down, blood from his eye socket sliding down the fence's mesh.

The dead person's companions didn't even seem to notice him dying. Jack approached the next guy and jabbed the pitchfork through his throat. The infected gurgled, but he still continued trying to reach Jack. Only when he lost enough blood or choked – Jack wasn't sure which one of those it was – did the infected fall dead. He would wake up again soon as an undead, slower and unable to make loud noise, but he would still go after his prey – unless Jack destroyed the brain.

He finally moved onto the woman. By then, another infected in the distance had seen the commotion and was on his way to the property, but Jack paid no attention to them. The woman at the fence looked surprisingly clean. She had no bite marks on her. No blood. Not even dirt. She could have fooled anyone that she was still alive had the putrid smell not accompanied her.

The woman wasn't infected. She was undead. For a moment, Jack wondered how she died. If she had no bite marks, it meant that she died in a different way. Maybe she had a small scratch somewhere and that's how she got infected, but she definitely wasn't running around chasing people before dying and resurrecting, because she would have had torn clothes and skin. The infected were careless about their own safety.

Jack imagined for a moment the woman just barely surviving a close encounter with an undead, only to find out that she had been infected. He wondered how she would have felt in that moment. Did she decide to commit suicide when she learned what would happen to her? Or maybe she swallowed a handful of pills when this all started just to avoid dying a gruesome death of being devoured alive? Where did she come from? Did she have a family?

Those questions had plagued Jack since the first day he and Linda went to Eugene to get the meds. He had punched a man senselessly – and maybe even killed him – and then he might have possibly killed the woman who was on the hood of the car, but he hadn't thought about it until later.

That day, when they arrived home, Jack wondered who those people were. What if the woman was a mother, and her children were waiting for her to come back home, but then she got infected and killed? That thought caused Jack to puke out his dinner.

But then he simply stopped thinking about it. He saw the infected and the undead as a threat and nothing more. He told himself that they were no longer human. But now, as he stared at this woman who was undead, and he had an undead wife inside his house, he couldn't help but notice his own hypocrisy.

Deciding that those thoughts were driving him crazy, Jack thrust the pitchfork forward and stabbed the woman through the eye, ending her hunger. She fell onto the grass, staining it with red. The next one was already on his way, but the others were still oblivious to the human at the farm.

Jack whistled to get their attention. They looked around in confusion, some of them turning their heads toward the woods, some looking at the sky. Jack continued whistling a tune until they all saw him and started moving in the direction of the farm.

"Breakfast, boys!" Jack shouted.

****

By the time Jack was done skewering all of the undead, he was sweating and panting. Dead bodies littered the front of the fence, and Jack knew that he needed to clear them out before the smell got unbearable and potentially attracted unwanted attention.

He had already smoked one cigarette, and he desperately wanted another one, but he only had four remaining. He suppressed the urge to smoke and went back to the porch where he returned the pitchfork stained with fresh blood. He then took the gate key out of his pocket and unlocked the padlock.

The gate opened outward, and there were bodies blocking it, so Jack had to shove hard until the gap was wide enough for him to sidle through. He then grabbed the corpses by their ankles and dragged them to the side until he could open the fence. He felt a twinge in his lower back, reminding him to maintain a correct posture when handling heavy stuff.

Once the gate was open, he went inside to grab his revolver. He then went back outside and around the side of the house toward his parked pickup truck. The red paint had been scraped off badly on the left side, and the bumper had a dent in it. For most of the time since the whole chaos started, the vehicle had remained parked under the rusty metal roofing that Jack had made himself, and yet despite that, the car was dirty as hell. The windshields were so dirty with mud and blood that Jack couldn't even see inside the car.

He had to wipe the windshields with water and detergent first, and once he did that, he got the urge to wash the entire truck. He would do it later, because now, he needed to transport the dead into the woods, and they would only make the back of his truck dirtier.

Jack stepped inside the car, placed the gun on the passenger's seat, and turned the key in the ignition. The engine whirred to life smoothly, immediately causing low vibrations inside the vehicle. Jack made sure to turn the car on for a few minutes at least once a week to prevent the battery from draining.

He drove the truck to the front of the property, and then killed the engine. He went outside, and then closed and locked the gate. He went back to the truck, lowered the railing on the back, and began working. Heaving the bodies into the back of the truck was difficult. Jack was used to heavy physical labor from working in construction before getting a job at the antique shop, but he hadn't done too many heavy things in the past few months, and that immediately became apparent on his stamina.

After loading four bodies into the back of the truck, he had to take a break. He then deduced that there was no more room for other bodies, so he closed the railing and decided that he would make two more trips after this.

He drove the truck to the edge of the woods and parked in reverse just in front of the tree line. He could have just left the bodies in front of the farm, but he didn't like the idea of having his own personal pile of dead bodies to taint his view every day.

Once he turned the key and the ignition stopped roaring, he waited to see if anything would come running at him. He scanned the thicket, trying to detect any kind of movement in the dark woods. It seemed peaceful, but then again, the undead shambled, so they could easily be missed.

Jack took the gun and opened the door, and immediately, the loud chirping of the birds filled his ears. The sound was pleasant. It reminded him of the times when he and Linda went berry and mushroom picking in these woods. He missed those days. Maybe one of these days, he could take Linda out into the woods, for old times' sake.

Jack whistled, his tune bouncing and echoing between the trees. He waited another protracted moment, but nothing came. No undead, no infected. That was good enough for him. He put the handgun in the back pocket of his jeans and lowered the railing of the truck again. The first thing he did was drag all the bodies out onto the ground. He wasn't overly careful with them. He grabbed them by whatever the closest limb was and tugged until they slumped on the grass.

Once the pickup was empty, Jack whistled again, and then once he was sure that he was alone, he dragged the bodies deeper into the woods one by one. When he first did this, he thought about driving the bodies all the way out to the road and leaving them there, but that was too much work and the gas was scarce.

He went about three hundred feet into the forest when he smelled, and then saw, the bloated and rotting remains of his previous batch. Most of the bodies still retained a human-like shape, but a lot of them were badly disfigured from the injuries they had suffered before dying permanently. Worms wiggled in their orifices, feasting on dead tissue and slowly disintegrating the flesh.

The smell was unbearable. Jack had to strain in order to stop himself from gagging. When this all started, Jack had thought about burning the bodies, but that would waste precious gas, and it might draw unwanted eyes to the farm.

Jack tossed the fresh body on top of the haphazard pile of the previous batch, and then went to retrieve the next one. Once all the bodies from the pickup were on the pile, he went back to the front of the farm.

The infected that he killed by stabbing him in the throat had already risen as an undead and was reaching for Jack from the ground.

"Ah, Christ." Jack rolled his eyes. He was too lazy to go back inside and grab the pitchfork, so he instead stomped the undead's head with the heel of his boot until the skull cracked and the creature stopped moving.

He then continued his work. Jack piled the bodies in the pickup, drove them to the edge of the woods, and unloaded them with the others. He sighed at the thought of having to do this at least once more.

All this time, he was looking for something to occupy himself, and now when he found it, he complained that it was given to him. It took him half an hour to get all the bodies onto the mound. He counted them along with the decomposing ones. There were around forty dead bodies. He tried to remember how many bodies there were in each batch. The first one was only two bodies, then five, then eight, if he remembered correctly. Then another small one, but now it was eleven. That wasn't good.

Lately, he'd seen the undead traveling in big hordes, and that worried him. There was a really big horde a few weeks ago that walked past the meadow and disappeared in the woods. There must have been at least a hundred of them, and that was not counting the ones in the woods that Jack couldn't even see.

What usually happened was the hordes left a few stragglers behind who got distracted by something and then didn't catch up with their group. More and more stragglers showed up at Jack's farmstead lately, and he knew that there was a risk that a big horde might run directly into his farm. If a hundred of those bastards piled on top of the fence, it wouldn't hold and the farm would be overrun.

Jack would need to do something about that risk – either set up some traps, or something that would redirect them from the farm. He wondered for a moment why they moved in groups like that. Maybe the ones at the front simply walked in a random direction and the others followed? No, this seemed more organized. As if they knew exactly where they were going. That scared him, but also gave him some hope, because it meant that they might really be capable of some deeper thinking than just how to fill their bellies.

Leaving the fresh batch of bodies for the maggots' buffet, he turned around and left the woods, feeling like he would need to shower with bleach in order to get the disgusting smell of death and the dirt of the bodies off him.

Once he was back inside the property, he parked the truck in the designated spot and locked the gate. He didn't even realize how vulnerable he felt outside in the woods until the padlock clicked in place. Jack used to love going out into the great outdoors. Now, everything beyond the fence seemed homicidal. Walking in the woods with Linda suddenly seemed like a terrible idea. No, he would not put her in danger like that. They were safe in here – for now.

But that didn't mean they always would be. Jack would need to go for a supply run, and very soon, because food for Linda was running out.

Chapter Seven

There was something about sharing a life with the person who you considered your soulmate. It wasn't about self-preservation anymore. Every breath you took was not just for yourself, but for your soulmate. You lived so that your soulmate could live.

"This is not a drill. Stay inside your homes and wait for further instructions from your local police," the man on the TV said. "In case you suspect that you or your loved ones might be–"

Jack flipped to the next channel. It showed a helicopter-view toward the city where chaos ensued. People were as tiny as ants from there and ran in various directions, fires burned, gunshots resounded, corpses littered the street, figures broke in and out of glass displays of the shops… Jack changed the channel again.

This one showed only static.

"Anything?" Linda asked as she finished pulling the blinds down on the windows and approaching the sofa where Jack sat. She held the phone up to her ear. Jack shook his head before changing the channel.

This one showed one of those colorful striped screens with a loud buzzing sound. The message "LOCK YOUR DOORS, CLOSE YOUR WINDOWS, AND DO NOT LET ANYONE INSIDE" stood in the middle of the screen.

"Nothing," Jack said.

"The phones aren't working," Linda said with worry in her tone as she hung up. "I'm worried about my parents."

"I'm sure they're fine, babe." He approached her and gave her a peck on the forehead. She wrapped her arms around his waist. She felt somewhat cold, probably still traumatized from the events earlier at Eugene. Jack said, "Everything's gone crazy. Going out to Eugene was a horrible idea. We could have died, I'm so sorry, babe."

Linda pulled slightly away and looked at him.

"What about your folks, Jack?" she asked solicitously.

"When I spoke to them a few hours ago, they were headed for the military checkpoint in Creswell," Jack said.

"I hope they're okay," she said.

She paced around the room while cradling herself. The TV still displayed the same warning message. Jack pulled out his phone and noticed that his internet was still working. He quickly entered all the social media apps that worked, and naturally, they were flooded with news about the living dead. Even checking the recommended news articles, he saw only apocalypse-related things. He reckoned that the internet would stop working soon.

"Jesus." Jack ran a hand down his mouth.

"What are we going to do?" Linda asked.

"Exactly what the message says. We'll keep the gate and the house locked, and we'll be safe that way. We won't let anyone inside, and we'll wait for all this to blow over."

"What if it doesn't blow over?"

"It will. You heard it on the radio earlier in the car. They said that they're organizing military evacuations."

Linda took a step back and fiddled with her fingers. She looked at the TV momentarily, and then at Jack. "Maybe we should go to one of those checkpoints," Linda said. "We'd be a lot safer with the army protecting us."

"Maybe. But everybody's probably going there, too. We could run into a lot of trouble until then. The freeway is probably backed up from everybody and their mothers trying to get there. That probably means a lot more infected over there."

Linda looked down and sighed. Jack got closer to her and put his hands on her cheeks. "We'll be fine here, babe. I promise. We just need to wait until this is all over. We have enough food and water. We got a backup generator in case the power goes out. We'll be fine. Trust me."

Linda ogled him for a moment, as if trying to decide if she should believe him or not.

"Okay, Jack," she said. "I trust you."

Chapter Eight

On the one hand, Jack felt lucky to still have his revolver and the bullets. On the other hand, he really missed his rifle. Although it wasn't as useful as the revolver in tight spaces, it gave him a sense of security. Now that it was gone, he would need to make do with just the revolver and hope for the best.

The first thing Jack did was open the wardrobe where he kept the ammo. He stuffed twelve extra bullets in his jacket's pockets and made sure that the revolver was fully loaded before putting it back in his jeans. He took a bottle of water, as well as a can of baked beans, just in case he lingered in the town for whatever reason. Sometimes, groups of the infected walked through the town, and he needed to lie low until they were gone. He put the food and water in the backpack, and then slithered into the shoulder straps of the backpack.

He put the supplies in the truck, and then decided that it was time to inform Linda where he was going. Would she respond to him? No. Would she understand him? He liked to believe so.

Jack sauntered toward the coop and grabbed the closest chicken. It managed to wiggle out of his grip, causing him to curse under his breath. By then, the chicken ran all the way into the opposite corner, and although a different chicken was closer, Jack had decided that he wanted to sacrifice the one that so foolishly dared to defy him. He opened the gate and stepped inside before walking over to the chicken and raising it, holding a firmer grip on it. The chicken didn't try running away this time.

He walked upstairs and unlocked Linda's room. She stood facing him, her chin lowered, but her pale eyes fixated on him. Whenever he entered the room, she stood. Jack had never seen her lying or sitting. She never slept, either. Whenever he leaned his ear on the door in the middle of the night when waking up to use the bathroom, he heard Linda's wheezing, and sometimes shuffling.

"Hey, baby," Jack said with a smile.

He was glad that Linda wasn't trying to attack him every time he entered. Sometimes, she'd go wild, and that's when he knew that she was really hungry. But most of the time these days, she would stare at him reticently as she did now.

The first time it happened, Jack was overcome with gaiety, because Linda being docile meant that he was making progress with her. He had wanted to come close to her and hug her, but the rancid stench emanating from her was what stopped him – not because he was disgusted, but because it reminded him that Linda wouldn't hesitate to take a bite out of his flesh.

He had seen that nearly happen in the past. When he first locked her in the room, he couldn't stand being away from her. He tried approaching her, but the moment his fingertips got in her vicinity, she angrily snapped her jaw at him, trying to taste him.

Jack was tempted to let her.

"You're probably wondering why I'm here so early," Jack said. Linda's eyes gravitated to the chicken. "I'm going to have to go to Eugene to find food. Okay?"

Linda responded by inhaling a sharp breath, and then wheezing it out. She was focused too much on the chicken because she knew that it was going to be her meal. Jack grabbed the chicken with both hands and tossed it where he usually tossed them toward the corner of the room. The chicken flapped its wings, and instantly, Linda went from lethargic to frenetic. Her eyes widened, she bared her teeth, and she threw herself on top of the chicken. The chicken clucked loudly and ran to the opposite corner of the room, dodging Linda by mere inches.

Linda was fast. She never once took her eyes off the chicken. She jumped toward the bird, and this time, managed to grab it by the wing, squeezing firmly. Feathers flew as the chicken vigorously flapped its free wing, but Linda had already sunk her teeth into its back.

The sounds of violent chewing and quick, heaving breaths filled the air. Jack waited a moment, and then pulled the key out of his pocket. He approached Linda, raised the chain that held her in place, and inserted the key into the lock on her back.

One smooth spin caused the lock to release its grip and fall on the ground with a loud thud. Linda, seemingly unaware, continued gnawing at the chicken. Jack put the key back in his pocket and backtracked to the chair where *The Witch of the Woods* sat.

"I'm going to leave the door open for you so you can walk around most of the house, okay?" he asked as he took the book and sat on the chair.

He opened the book to the page where he last stopped reading the story. So far in the story, the main characters, a boy and a girl named Will and Zara became best friends and decided to take a shortcut through the woods one day after they were done picking berries. Their parents had warned them not to go through the woods, but Will and Zara knew that they wouldn't make it before nightfall, so they decided to cut through the woods instead. They got lost, and night was almost upon them. They met an old lady – a witch – who offered to help them find their way back.

"Remember where we stopped with the story, babe?" Jack asked.

Linda had bitten into the chicken and then jerked her head back, tearing a particularly tough piece of meat off the dead animal. Jack closed the book and stood up.

"I'll leave the book for you here, in case you decide to read it," he said and plopped the book back on the chair. "I can't let you out in the yard because of the chickens, but you can walk anywhere you want in the house. I'll be back as soon as I can, okay? I love you."

No response. Jack sighed. He wished that he could get a response from Linda. Just one simple response, of any kind. He turned around and walked out of the room.

He double-checked if all the windows were closed so that Linda didn't get injured by accident. Jack also locked the pantry. He knew that the canned goods wouldn't interest Linda, but she might end up knocking the cans over, and he spent a long time sorting them meticulously.

Jack locked the backdoor and pulled the blinds on the kitchen windows, because he didn't want Linda seeing the chicken coop outside. If she saw it, she'd go through the window even if she sliced herself to bits, just to get to the chickens.

By the time he was done double-checking everything, the shuffling upstairs had stopped. Linda had finished her meal. Jack wondered if she would even bother to get out of the room. He was slightly worried about safely restraining her once he was back, but Linda was his wife, and he knew how to deal with her. He hoped that a walk around the house might help her remember a little of herself. An unsettling voice at the back of his mind spoke to him.

What are you hoping for? You'll never be able to have a normal life with her like this. Things will never go back to the way they were before.

"Shut up," he said aloud to the voice.

The voice was wrong. Jack was not going to give up on his wife. Before he could entertain any other morbid thoughts, he strode out of the house and locked the front door. He stepped off the porch and looked at the second-floor windows. He couldn't see anything inside. He wondered where Linda was right now.

He then drove the truck outside the property, then closed and locked the gate behind him. As he got in his truck, he looked in the rearview mirror toward the house. He thought he could see the slim silhouette of his wife slinking past the window in the living room.

"I'll be back soon, honey," Jack muttered to himself as he stepped on the gas pedal.

Chapter Nine

Home wasn't a place for him anymore. It was a person. Wherever he went, he would be home, as long as he was with her.

"Great, the power just went out," Linda exclaimed when she tried to flip the light switch on.

It was still only noon, and Jack wouldn't have noticed the difference had the TV's screen not gone blank. Not that there was anything to see there, anyway. It had only been four days since they went to Eugene, and already most of the communication channels were dead.

The phones weren't working, so they couldn't even check if their family and friends were okay. The TV channels weren't broadcasting anything, so the question was whether the government was even doing anything to organize an evacuation. Even the radio, which was riddled with groups of people setting up their own channels, now dwindled to only three that shared no relevant information.

"I guess we won't be using the stove anymore then," Jack said.

Linda ran a hand through her hair, her nostrils flaring in frustration. She then put her hands on her hips and stared into empty space, as if pondering how to fix this situation. Jack knew that she would only become extremely annoyed from here on out, so he hopped to his feet to rectify the situation.

"Babe, this is what we expected would happen," he said as he approached her. "Look, we still have the backup generator. If it gets really bad, we can turn it on. Okay?"

Linda looked at him with a tired glare and nodded. Jack kissed her on the forehead and said, "I'm going to double check the breaker box to make sure it's not something on our end."

"Thanks," Linda said.

Jack went outside to the back of the house and opened the breaker box. Sure enough, one quick scrutiny of the fuses confirmed that the power outage came from whatever the source supplying them with power was. Jack scratched his cheek, feeling a little embarrassed that he didn't know more about electricity. Had he known more, he could have set up a wind turbine or something like that to power the farm. He closed the breaker box and returned inside.

"Yup, it's not the breaker box," Jack said as he entered the living room.

Linda was seated on the couch where Jack usually sat. He slumped on the seat next to her and brushed the stray lock of hair out of her face. She looked at him wearily, her eyelids looking droopy.

"It'll be fine, babe," Jack said. "We just need to wait."

Linda nodded and leaned her head on his shoulder.

"I'm just going to take a short nap. I haven't slept all night."

Jack gave her a smooch on the forehead. He could feel Linda's breathing relaxing, and when he looked down, her eyes were closed.

"Sing for me," Linda whispered.

"Oh, come on. You know I'm a bad singer. I sound like a crow," Jack retorted.

"Then hum," Linda said.

"I don't hum," Jack said.

Linda looked at him. Her eyes were half-open, and she smiled. "I hear you humming when you think you're alone," she said.

"Y-you heard that?" he asked, his cheeks burning from embarrassment.

Linda slowly nodded, closing her eyes again.

"When did you hear it, exactly?" Jack asked.

"A few times. I sometimes hear you humming and then I freeze because I don't want to interrupt it."

Jack thought about all the times when he hummed. He only did it when he was alone – or thought he was alone – while doing chores. He also spoke to himself sometimes. He cringed at the thought of Linda hearing that.

"Well, come on. Hum for me," Linda patted his chest.

"I don't want to," Jack said.

Linda pushed away from him with alacrity and then said, "Fine. Then I'll just listen to the video I have on my phone."

"You have a… wait a second!"

Linda had already gotten up and was running toward the stairs with her phone out.

"Linda, stop!" Jack shouted and went after her.

Linda had already ascended the stairs, giggling mischievously. Jack followed her and heard distorted humming from somewhere upstairs. That didn't sound like him at all, but he knew that it was, based on the evil grin that Linda had plastered to her face.

"Linda, give me the phone," Jack outstretched a hand and curled his fingers toward himself.

Linda shook her head. The humming in the video sounded terrible. Jack needed to turn it off immediately. He jackknifed toward Linda. She screamed playfully and rushed inside the bedroom. By the time Jack entered, the humming had stopped, and Linda stood in the middle of the room with her hands behind her back.

"Linda. Baby. Love of my life. Give me the phone," Jack said.

"Choose a hand," she taunted him.

"Left," Jack said.

Linda presented an empty palm to Jack.

"Right," he said.

She showed the other hand, and it too, was empty.

"Okay, enough playing around," Jack said as he grabbed Linda and threw her on the bed.

She screamed, and then laughed. Jack touched her pockets, and then her rear, lingering for a moment on it despite not feeling the blocky outline of the phone. Linda slapped his hand away.

"Where's the phone?" Jack asked.

Linda shrugged. She had a tight-lipped smile on her face. Jack raised his head and looked around the room. The phone was nowhere in sight. He jerked his head back to Linda and said, "You know what? Fine, keep it. Civilization is collapsing, and we have no electricity. Once your phone runs out of power, it's game over."

"Maybe one day, archeologists will discover my phone and find a way to recharge it, and they'll find a video of you humming."

Jack squeezed his eyes shut at that unpleasant thought. "What a horrible thing to uncover," he said.

He slumped his head onto Linda's chest, where she continued to caress his cheek until they fell asleep.

Chapter Ten

Eugene wasn't far from the farm. Back before The Collapse, it took Jack ten minutes to get from the farm to the town with his truck. Now, as he drove on the overgrown road riddled with brown and golden leaves, swerving around the haphazardly abandoned cars that blocked the path, slowing down and checking his surroundings, Jack knew that it would take him much longer.

The sky had turned gray since he had left the farm, giving Jack a sense of foreboding. The feeling of dread further rose inside him the closer he got to Eugene. The leaves that had fallen onto the road dispersed under the gust of Jack's truck. He tried not to look at the mutilated and rotting corpses splayed on the road and inside the cars.

There was a lot to see that Jack didn't want to see out here. A man who was missing the entire lower part of his body lay on the hood of a truck crashed into a tree. A woman leaning her head on the steering wheel stared at Jack from inside her car with widely open eyes. She had a dent in her skull. Next to her, toddler's legs dangled upward from the front seat. Jack felt grateful for not being able to see how badly messed up the kid was. A man still strapped in his seat tried to reach out to Jack when he saw him driving past him, hissing and spitting. He had a bite mark on his exposed forearm and was missing two fingers on his hand.

Jack saw a couple of undead mindlessly roaming the streets. Upon seeing Jack's moving truck, they began shambling toward him. Jack swerved around the first two, and grazed the third one, causing the woman's arm to bend unnaturally with a loud crack. He looked in the rearview mirror and saw her still lumbering toward him.

The closer Jack got to Eugene, the worse it would be, he realized. With the town being more populated, he expected to find not just a plethora of walking corpses, but still living infected who had amazing motor abilities, and scavengers.

That last worried him the most. The last time he visited Eugene, it had been relatively quiet, save for a few undead aimlessly wandering the streets, detached from their fellow zombies. However, as he exited the supermarket, he heard gunshots and voices. Voices should have made him joyous, but instead, they caused him to panic, because these didn't sound like friendly voices.

He couldn't discern what they were saying, except for one sentence before an echoing gunshot resounded.

"Please, don't shoot, please!"

That forced Jack to scamper all the way to the street where he parked his truck and drive off with screeching tires. He constantly glanced in the rearview mirror until he was out of Eugene to see if anyone would be driving after him. Luckily, no one did.

Now that he had to go back to the town, getting caught by the remaining humans terrified him. It was evident that the town had been abandoned for the most part, and the ones who stayed were now in charge. That meant that there was no law to regulate what happened. That also meant that the scavengers would do everything in their power to protect their territory.

But what would they do to trespassers? Shoot on sight? Capture Jack, kill him, and put his meat in the freezer? He hoped that the people in Eugene – or anywhere else – hadn't progressed to the stage of cannibalism.

The first rows of the low buildings peeked between the trees at the far end of the road. As much as Jack wanted to drive directly into the town, he decided that the best course of action would be leaving the truck outside, sneaking in, and then making a quick getaway.

No undead or infected were in sight, which worked well to Jack's advantage. Once he was a hundred feet within the entrance of Eugene, he turned the truck around and killed the engine. He squinted at the rearview mirror, and then adjusted it so he could see the entrance to the town. A part of him expected to see figures in the distance patrolling the rooftops, but the town was quiet.

Jack needed a cigarette, and a cigarette he would have. If he got lucky, he would find more in the town. If not, then he would quit smoking. He stepped outside, pulled out one whole cigarette from his pack, and lit it. As soon as he inhaled the first whiff of smoke, relaxation surged through his body – just enough to get him ready for his supply run.

He exhaled the plume of smoke, watching it disperse into thin air. The entire time, he darted his eyes around the horizon, trying to detect any movements. So far so good. He felt about as nervous as the day he decided to propose to Linda.

He had organized a romantic dinner at *Rye*, and although he had no idea about French cuisine or anything romantic, all he knew was that he wanted to ask Linda the question. They had been dating for almost a year, and he still wasn't sure if she would say yes to the question, but the one thing he was sure of was that he wanted nothing more than to spend the rest of his life waking up next to Linda.

Linda looked even more beautiful that night than she ever had before. Jack was compelled to call her beautiful multiple times, causing her to blush at his clumsy attempts to compliment her. When the time came to ask the question, Jack fumbled with his words. Linda stared at him with a reserved smile, letting him dig his own grave.

Finally, Jack gave up and just pulled out the ring box and opened it to show the engagement ring to Linda. She gasped so loudly that the heads of the other guests turned to look at her. At the same time, she had a Cheshire cat smile on her face, and that gave Jack the boost of confidence that he desperately needed.

He got on one knee and began, "Linda, ever since I first laid my eyes on you, all I wanted was—"

"Yes!" Linda shouted before he could finish the sentence.

She leaped to kiss him, and the restaurant was filled with a reverberating applause. Jack hadn't even realized how quickly his heart had been beating until then. He felt as though he had just run a marathon. The rest of the dinner was a blur. The only thing Jack remembered was Linda's smile, and the way she flashed the ring, her smile widening every time she saw its glint.

The cigarette had burned to the filter much faster than Jack had expected it to. He dropped the butt on the ground and crushed it under his shoe. He took off his backpack and pulled out the water to take a sip. He was a little hungry, but he felt as though his stomach wouldn't be able to digest a bread crumb right now, so he returned the bottle and hoisted the backpack up. He double-checked his revolver, and decided to keep it in his hand for a quick action in case it became necessary.

Since everything he needed was ready, he turned to the town. He wouldn't bother taking the keys out of the ignition. His truck was surrounded by ramshackle vehicles, and the truck, dirty with blood and rust didn't stand out in such company. He hadn't planned on staying long, anyway.

It was time to enter Eugene.

As he took the first step, Jack couldn't help but think of Linda. Where was she right now? What was she doing? He hoped that she was walking around the house, finding familiar things. He then reminded himself that he needed to stay focused. One mishap could be the end of him – and that would also mean the end of Linda.

The building closest to the entrance – a long-since abandoned warehouse with broken windows – was upon Jack. Jack had approached the town by walking through tall grass. The grass rustled as he plodded through it, and with the absence of any other sounds, his approach was only further accentuated.

Since the undead usually swarmed the avenues and any bigger streets, Jack decided to take his chances through the alleyways as much as he could. Before he went onto the grueling task of sneaking through the town, he closed his eyes and tried to imagine the map of Eugene from a top-down point of view.

He was in the industrial zone close to the entrance, and the closest building that would have any supplies would be the small shop two blocks down. If that didn't have any meats that would appeal to Linda, he would need to go to the supermarket further down. That would be riskier, but it was sure to have supplies.

Jack opened his eyes and turned to walk toward the backside of the warehouse. The hand that white-knuckled the revolver was clammy, and Jack slightly released his grip on the firearm. Almost as soon as he entered the alley and made his way forward, he heard sounds – sounds that he was used to, but sounds that sent warning like the hiss of a snake.

Moaning, groaning, gasping, and wheezing draped the air. It sounded like there were dozens, possibly even hundreds of them. That made both relief and dread wash over him. If the undead were here, that meant that no humans were, but it meant that he still needed to deal with the undead.

Jack reached the end of the alley and peeked toward the avenue. A split second later, he retreated into the cover of the alley. There weren't hundreds of them, but still way too many for Jack to deal with. He counted at least fifteen on the street, and the problem was that they were so thinly spread that it was impossible to just go around them in a wide arc.

That route was not safe. Jack went back and then tried another alley. This time, he had more luck because the street only had two undead – an old lady with a broken ankle, and a teenager. Jack's gaze lingered on the teenager, because he thought he recognized him as the one he saw when he was with Linda – the one who shot the infected. When the undead turned sideways, partially revealing its face, Jack realized that it wasn't the same kid.

He tip-toed across the street and into the alleyway on the other side, where the face-down dead body of a woman rested. As Jack walked forward, he looked back to make sure he wasn't being followed. A hoarse scream under him caused him to jerk his head down.

The skinny, battered woman who he previously thought was just a dead body grabbed him by the ankle and was pulling herself closer to him, her half-rotted teeth flashing and ready to bite into fresh meat. Jack tugged the foot backward, but the woman's grip remained firm on him. Her eyes were fixated on his ankle. She had the same stare as did Linda when Jack brought her the chickens.

Seeing that caused him to yank his foot even harder. The woman's bony grip slipped from his ankle, and he took three steps back to put some distance from her. She clawed at the floor, trying to pull herself closer with her emaciated arms, but only causing her bloodied fingertips to leave a red trail on the concrete. She was still blocking Jack's path, and he had to take care of her.

He looked back once more. Still not being followed. Although the infected were more dangerous than the undead, the undead were still very, very deadly. Jack saw what they could do. When not hunting, they would shamble, and it made them look too weak to even stand, let alone hurt someone.

But as soon as they saw something alive, they seemed to kickstart into action. They were capable of running shorter distances – if their legs were still relatively intact – and they could even pounce their prey. Bullets to the body only seemed to make them flinch or slow them down, and sometimes, not even that. And if they attacked in groups…

Jack couldn't afford to waste time. He got closer to the woman on the ground, allowing her to grab his ankle. He raised his foot, and then brought it down with full force on the woman's head. The woman's head slammed against the pavement, but that didn't stop her from continuing to reel him in with her enfeebled grasp.

Jack brought his foot down again, harder this time. And then again.

A crack echoed in the alley, much louder than Jack hoped it would, and in his mind, he told himself that he might as well have just fired one bullet. Even after the crack, the woman raised her head again, but Jack continued stomping on her. More cracks, and the woman's skull concaved and she stopped moving entirely. The cracking was replaced by squelching sounds. Blood pooled around the woman's head, and only then did Jack cease his stomping spree.

He took a step back, looked up, and then pivoted his head around to make sure he hadn't attracted unwanted attention. The alley grew somewhat quiet. Jack looked at his boot. It was covered in blood, some of it going onto his jeans. He ignored that and stepped over the dead woman, trying not to look at the mess he had made of her skull.

Once Jack reached the end of the alley, he peeked onto the adjacent street. Although littered with corpses, none of them moved, much to his relief, because the supermarket was close to him. Before stepping out, he looked left and right down the streets once more, squinting to detect any movement as if his life depended on it – which it did.

The few cars that sat sorrowfully in the middle of the street were good for cover while crossing the street, so Jack took a mental note to duck behind them in case he ran into unwanted trouble. Jack glanced at the wristwatch Linda had gifted him for his birthday. Three twenty-four, it showed. It always showed three twenty-four.

Jack propelled himself forward and walked across the street in a crouching stance. Once he reached the charred, overturned car, he stopped, got down on one knee, and looked around once more.

Silence still hung in the air.

In fact, even the moaning sounds in the distance could not be heard from here. It should have made Jack feel peaceful, but the serenity never came. Instead, it was veiled by an ominous feeling that Jack couldn't quite describe. The only thing he likened to it was the calm before the storm. He hoped he was wrong.

Jack sneaked toward the supermarket just a little faster. He only stopped when he was a few feet in front of it. The tall panes of glass had long-since been destroyed, leaving millions of tiny shards on the ground that crunched beneath Jack's shoes. The interior was dark, the daylight just barely peering inside. Even in the dimness, Jack could see what disarray the supermarket was in. He hoped that he would still find something useful in there.

Ignoring the shards of glass that sounded loud enough to wake up the dead, Jack sauntered inside, holding the revolver pointed in front of him. Once he stopped moving, it grew deafeningly quiet in the supermarket. When he started moving again, the sound of glass bounced off the walls of the store.

Quickly in, quickly out. Come on, Jack.

Jack walked down the aisle toward the deli section, making sure to avoid the aisles that had corpses splayed in them. It felt weird to see the supermarket in such a state – devoid of life, light, sounds, and in a mess. Jack had been buying groceries here for years ever since they opened the place in 2012, and he had always known it as a place brimming with people pushing their shopping carts, the beeping at the cash registers, the smelly section where they sold the fish, the cold section that sold dairy products and frozen goods, and so on.

Now, derelict and collapsing into the dust of its former magnificence, the supermarket looked as if hundreds of years had passed, and not a few months. Jack couldn't help but feel a sadness creeping up on him when he realized how quickly it takes for something to fall into such a state of abandonment. He couldn't be sure if the government was doing something to mitigate this situation, but if the rest of the country was in the same state as Eugene, then it would only be a matter of time before every other building in the country fell into oblivion like the supermarket, until they collapsed entirely and nature reclaimed the land.

Jack had made it to the deli section, so he took off his backpack and unzipped it. He held it in one hand, while still clutching the revolver in the other. Most of the food on the shelves had been pilfered, and the stuff that remained was maggot-infested meat behind the glass stand. Some dried goods remained, but Jack didn't harbor any hopes of them still being edible.

Still, he decided to take his chances, and then he would visit some other stores if he had the opportunity. He swept the sausages, the jerkies, the bacons, and other packaged stuff into his backpack. It had grown relatively heavy, even though it wasn't a lot of food – three, maybe four-days-worth of food for his wife.

Jack zipped his backpack halfway, and then he stopped. He perked up his ears, and that's when he heard it.

Voices at the entrance.

Masculine voices spoke to each other jovially, their voices carrying all the way to Jack. Jack felt his heart leaping into his throat. *People*. He zipped up his bag, slowly to avoid making lots of noise, and heaved it on his back. The voices were getting closer, and now Jack could partially discern what they were saying.

"–said "Please don't, I'll tell you what you want", and I was like, "Nah, man. You ain't got nothin' to offer", and I shot him in the balls."

Laughter erupted in the supermarket. Jack tip-toed in a crouching position behind one of the aisles and glanced toward the entrance. He could see the elongated shadows of people cast on the floor, as they walked in Jack's direction, before getting swallowed by the dark. Jack made his way from the deli section to the canned goods stand to put some distance from the people. If he could skirt around them by using the aisles for cover, he could get out of the store without getting spotted. What worried him was that there might be more people waiting outside the store.

Should he hide and wait for them to leave? Should he shoot his way through? Jack felt cold sweat enveloping him.

"So, he was still alive after you shot him?" a voice asked.

"Yeah," the one from before answered. "He was screaming like a little bitch the entire time. I didn't want to kill him right away. We already killed his sister while they were running, and I wanted to give him time for that information to settle."

"You're a real psycho, man."

Jack heard crashing sounds coming from the direction of the voices. That was good, because as long as they made noise, he would know where they were and would be safe. He prudently stepped around the items scattered on the floor, careful not to kick any of them. A corpse of a man in a suit was in his way, slumped with its back against the ice cream fridge, which made Jack pause.

He couldn't tell if the corpse was actually a corpse, or an undead, and the last thing he needed was to have another wrestling session like he did in the alley and attract attention.

"No, we didn't end up feeding him to the undead. We strung his corpse in front of the base as a warning," the voice said.

The matter-of-fact kind of way he spoke sounded like he was talking about a crazy night out drinking and not killing a human being. The fact that he spoke with such cold-bloodedness about killing another person made Jack sick to his stomach. These people were monsters, no better than the infected who hunted and ate them.

Jack sidled past the dead body, carefully watching the blood-covered bald head. Sure enough, the moment he looked away, a groan escaped the man's mouth. Jack looked back at the corpse. The man's head was raised, and he drunkenly watched Jack, but made no attempt to reach him.

"Wait. You guys hear that?" one of the voices asked.

That was Jack's cue to leave. He continued toward the entrance, faster, but trying to remain as quiet as possible. He gripped the gun so firmly that his hand started to hurt.

"Came from over there, let's check it out," another voice said.

With that came the resounding footsteps in the supermarket. It was difficult to tell where exactly they were coming from and how close they were. Jack reached the end of the aisle with his gun pointed in front of him, but he didn't want to just jump out, even though the exit was only a dozen or so feet away. He peeked toward the street. His escape was so close.

"Over here!" one of the men shouted. A deafening bang exploded in the supermarket. Jack felt something whistling past his ear, and only a moment later, he realized that it was a bullet. He jackknifed toward the exit as more gunshots ensued. Things shattered under the bullets' impact all around Jack, but he didn't stop. For all he knew, he might have been shot and the adrenaline was pushing him to run without feeling pain.

"Shoot him!" someone shouted as more gunshots ensued.

Jack ran across the glass-littered floor. He had made it outside. He veered to the left to break the line of sight with his pursuers, and then he bumped into a figure. Jack practically bounced back and fell on his rear.

Before he could figure out what was going on, a baseball bat connected with his temple, and then everything went dark.

Chapter Eleven

He could tell how she felt before even she knew it herself. It was the small things she unconsciously did that gave her away – like the way she turned away from him whenever she was angry, or the way she pressed tightly against him when she was sad, or the way she smiled when she was affectionate. It worked the other way around, too. She knew exactly how he felt at any given moment even when he tried to hide it. They were two halves that needed each other to be whole.

"Hello?! Anybody home?!" the muffled voices boomed outside.

Jack woke up with a start. It was dark outside. He had fallen asleep on Linda's chest earlier that day after their joke-fight with the phone, but how they managed to lose an entire day was beyond him.

"Someone! Please! We need help!" the voice shouted again.

"Who is that?" Linda asked timorously.

Jack couldn't see her face in the dark, but he imagined her eyes to be wide as saucers.

"I don't know," Jack said as he stood up and cautiously approached the window.

He immediately saw three figures standing at the gate. There were other figures in the distance behind them, and even in the dark, Jack could tell based on their lamely hanging arms and outstretched arms that they were the undead. Linda joined Jack at the window, following his gaze over his shoulder.

"Somebody! Please! They're coming after us!" a different voice said this time.

"Jack, we have to help them!" Linda said.

"No. We don't know them," Jack shook his head. "They could be dangerous."

"Come on!" the voice outside shouted. "My son is only nine!"

Jack looked at the figures again. One of them was much smaller than the other two. A child, Jack realized. The figures on the meadow behind them were getting closer. They were no more than fifty feet away from them now, and although they were shambling, they were closing the distance between them and their prey fast.

"Jack, please. We need to let them in." Linda grabbed him by the wrist.

Jack looked at her darkened face, and then outside at the figures. They were spinning intermittently, glancing from the farm to the pursuers. They had a child. Jack couldn't let a child die, and that was ultimately the only thing that tipped the scales in his decision.

He raced downstairs, grabbed his rifle from the wardrobe, and unlocked the front door. Linda followed him closely behind, but gave him enough space to navigate the house.

Once the door was opened, a squall of cold air swaddled Jack's face. The violent groaning and screeching were close. Jack hopped off the porch and ran toward the fence, simultaneously pulling the key out of his pocket.

He still couldn't see the people in front of his house clearly, but there was no time to scrutinize them. Jack put the key in the padlock and turned it. The gate was unlocked.

"Oh, thank you, mister!" one of the people said.

"Jack!" Linda shouted.

Jack looked toward the meadow to see an infected sprinting toward the boy. Jack raised his rifle, aimed it at the attacker's head, and squeezed the trigger. A bang echoed in the air and Jack's rifle kicked upward. The head of the infected jerked to the side and he fell sideways like a bag of potatoes, where he ceased moving.

"Get inside!" Jack shouted as he pushed the gate open.

The three figures squeezed inside just as another infected reached Jack, all the while screeching at the top of his lungs. Jack fired another round. This one went through the throat of the infected. Its head jerked backward and its legs violently kicked up into the air for a moment before it fell on its back, as if yanked from behind by the neck by an invisible cord. The undead clawed at his throat and gurgled for a moment, while the blood spurted out, before all movement ceased entirely.

Jack closed the gate and frenetically locked it before more of the infected could approach. He turned the key in the padlock and stepped back just when the fence rattled violently. A woman pressed her face against the mesh, snapping her teeth like a crocodile and hissing at Jack.

"Inside, now," Jack commanded, not taking his eyes off the infected woman.

The slower ones were now approaching the property, their arms outstretched in front of them, their mouths probably salivating at the prey in front of them. Jack wouldn't deal with them now. The fence would hold against them anyway.

He turned around and guided the figures inside the house. Linda was already on her way to light a candle to illuminate the living room. Jack closed the front door behind him, muffling the outside screams and moans. The blinds were already down on the first floor, so they didn't need to worry about being watched through the windows.

"Everybody okay?" Jack asked.

A dim orange glow erupted from the coffee table, illuminating the center of the living room. Linda blew on the match to extinguish it and gestured to the couch. "Please, sit. Make yourselves at home," she said with a smile.

"Thank you," one of the men said.

Jack could see the features on the people more clearly now. One of them was around Jack's age, even though he had a receding hairline. The other one – the taller and bulkier one – was in his late thirties by Jack's assumption. The smaller figure was a child, just as Jack had assumed when staring out the window. Under the candlelight, the boy looked pallid, the shadows on his face exacerbating the catatonic look on him.

"You saved our lives, thank you, folks," the one with the receding hairline said as he sat on the couch. "I'm Nolan. This here is my brother, Chris." He pointed to the bulky guy. "And this is my son, Nathan." Pointing to his son.

"Nice to meet you," Linda said. "I'm Linda. This is my husband, Jack."

The adults all shook hands, but Jack refused to let go of the rifle. Chris guided the boy to the couch and had him sit, and then he sat next to him. Jack felt relatively safe with all three of them huddled together like that, because he could keep an eye on them.

"Hi, Nathan. I'm Linda." Linda smiled as she leaned on her knees and bent down to be on the same eye level as the boy.

Nathan looked down in response.

"Don't mind him. He's still in shock," Nolan said. "He uh… his mother was attacked by a group of those crazies, and he uh… well, let's just say he saw every gruesome detail," Nolan's tone turned somber toward the end.

"That's so horrible. I can't imagine how difficult things must have been for you guys," Linda said. "You must be hungry and thirsty."

"We sure could use some water, ma'am. We've been on the run from those freaks since early afternoon," Nolan said.

Linda immediately went into the pantry. Jack sat on the edge of the sofa. He placed the butt of his rifle on the floor and sniffled. "Where do you guys come from?" he asked.

"Corvallis," Chris spoke up with a gruff voice. "We heard about them checkpoints that the military's been organizing. There was one just North of Portland in Clatskanie, but it's too close to the big city, so we went South in hopes of reaching the checkpoint in Veneta."

"There's a military checkpoint in Veneta?" Jack frowned.

Linda returned with three bottles of water and three cans of something. She gave each of them a bottle and a can, making sure to do it in an extra amicable way toward Nathan. The kid took the bottle and the can, but refused to look at Linda. She tousled his hair and went to stand next to Jack.

"That's what the radio's been talking about for a while. But then they stopped broadcasting, the sons of bitches." Chris shook his head. "They might be all dead for all we know. Fuck."

Jack and Linda exchanged a glance. Jack could immediately tell that she was intrigued by this because the way she stared at him in a focused manner.

"Language," Nolan reprimanded Chris.

"Oh, come on, Nolan." Chris scoffed. "You just watched your wife get picked to the bone by those freaks, the world is burning, and you care about your son learning new swear words? To fucking hell with that!"

Tension instantly seemed to fill the air. It was evident that Chris was edgy because of everything he had seen out there.

"So, we're supposed to give up and become like those folks who were killing each other for antibiotics?" Nolan asked. "The world might be burning, but we're still here."

Chris' lips tightened. He looked like he was about to get up and punch Nolan, but then his face went slack. Linda spoke to break the silence a moment later. "We're only half an hour away from Veneta. Jack, do you think we should go there?"

Jack looked down at the darkened floor for a moment, deep in thought. He looked up and then shook his head. "Too dangerous. You saw how messed up the roads to Eugene were. It's probably worse toward Veneta," he said.

"But we won't be taking the freeway," she said and then looked at the guests. "If you guys are headed there, then we can give you a lift–"

"Linda," Jack interrupted her sternly. Linda went quiet.

Chris glowered at Jack – or maybe it was the dim light of the candle that made him look like he was angry. Nolan inhaled a deep breath through his nose and said,

"That's alright, folks. We're heading there anyway, even if we have to walk."

Silence descended upon the room. The moaning and the rattling of the fence outside could be heard, but just barely. Linda opened her mouth. She was probably about to disagree with the group putting themselves in danger by walking to Veneta, but she then looked at Jack and closed her mouth. Usually, the two of them could read each other's faces without speaking. That was really useful in case they found themselves in situations that they wanted to avoid.

Oh, you want us to join you for drinks this week? Jack, what do you think? Do we have any plans then? Linda would ask and then turn to face him. If she smiled, it meant that she wanted to go, but she wanted to make sure Jack was also okay with it. If she had a rictus, then he would know that he should make an excuse.

"Look, I can give you a ride for a portion of the way there," Jack said, deciding to meet Linda halfway. "But I can't go too far toward Veneta. It's too dangerous."

"Come on, man. We have a child with us." Chris upturned his palms. "What kind of person would let a chi—"

"No, we completely understand, mister," Nolan interrupted as he shot a stern glare in Chris' direction. "We don't expect you to play a cab driver, at least not during these times. But would it be too much if we asked to stay the night? We'd be out of here by mornin'."

Jack and Linda exchanged another glance. The way the corners of her eyebrows arched upward told Jack that she wanted to let them stay. He didn't want to agree, but he couldn't resist that look. Jack sighed deeply.

"Okay. One night. We'll give you food and water and some meds if you need any. Believe me, folks, I'd love nothing more than to have you here until this whole thing blows over, but we're a little scarce on supplies, too."

Out of the corner of his eye, Jack could see Chris frowning at him. As soon as their eyes met, Chris' glance gravitated to the table.

"Everything is fine, friend," Nolan smiled. "Just tonight, and then we'll be out of here."

But Jack was focused on Chris. Something about the look in his eyes worried him.

Chapter Twelve

"Hey. Hey, dumbass. Wake the fuck up," a disembodied voice said from somewhere.

Jack floated through nothingness for a moment, but then his surroundings began to crystalize. He heard the voice more clearly, and he became aware of the throbbing in his head.

"Hey, fucker. I'm talking to you," the voice said again.

Jack felt gentle slaps on his cheek. He opened his mouth to say something, but only a gasp escaped his mouth. He forced himself to open his eyes. It felt as if he was trying to open a pair of badly rusted windows. The image in front of him was blurry, so Jack squeezed his eyes shut in a momentary blink.

The picture cleared up and he saw a person standing in front of him. His features were still unclear, and Jack had to blink a few more times to get a better look. The first thing he became aware of was the dirty face with needly beard and crooked teeth standing in front of him. The guy had greasy shoulder-length hair and wore a thick torn jacket and had dusty jeans. Although he looked much older, he couldn't have been more than twenty, Jack realized.

The second thing Jack became aware of was the room he was located in. It was a small concrete room, damp and smelling of must. Natural light came in from somewhere, but Jack couldn't tell from where. On the other side of the room, leaning against the door, was a towering figure of a man in a coat. He had distinctly blue eyes above an unkempt, bushy beard. He held an assault rifle in his hands and chewed on something while smiling connivingly at Jack. Next to him was a woman with bedraggled hair, her arms crossed as she shot Jack a spiteful look. She had a handgun in the pocket of her pants.

The third and final thing Jack became aware of was the fact that he was seated on a chair, and that his hands were behind his back. He tried moving them, but was met with resistance.

"Don't fight it too hard, my man," the young guy said, "You'll hurt yourself."

The two behind laughed. The young guy straightened his back and put his hands on his hips. He smacked his lips and shook his head while looking down at Jack.

"Where the hell did you come from, anyway? We swept the entire town, and we never found nobody hiding. So, where'd you come from?"

Jack refused to respond. He fought against his restrains, but the harder he did so, the more they dug into his skin and abraded his wrists.

"I see. You're one of them tough guys, ain't ya?" the young one asked. He rubbed his hands together, smiling widely. Jack saw that he was missing one canine tooth.

"Now, here's how things work here," the kid said. "You give us some useful information, like where to find some food, water, weapons, whatever. We go and check it out, and if we like what we find, we let you go. If we don't or if you lie to us..." The guy leaned on his knees so that he was eye to eye with Jack. "We strip you naked and throw you to the biters." He paused for a moment, enough for Jack to feel his stale breath. "So, what do you say?"

Jack looked at the other two in the room. The tall guy with the assault rifle looked amused by the whole thing. The woman conveyed boredom.

"Hey, eyes on me, pretty boy," the young guy said, gently slapping Jack.

Jack looked at him. "Go fuck yourself," he said spitefully.

The guy retained the fixed grimace on his face, and then nodded. He straightened his back again, looked at the ceiling, and then swung his fist out of nowhere. The knuckles connected with Jack's cheek, sending searing pain in his already painful head. The guy punched him over and over, hitting Jack's temple, his cheek, his nose, his forehead. His entire face hurt from the punches, but he refused to cry out in pain in front of his kidnappers.

By the time the young guy stopped batting, he was winded, and Jack had to spit blood out of his mouth. He ran his tongue across all teeth to make sure they were still there. They were.

"Okay, listen, asshole," the captor said. "We can do this the easy way or the hard way." He reached behind his back and pulled something out before putting it in front of Jack's face. Jack saw the glint of a pocket knife flashing in front of him, causing him to recoil as much as his binds allowed him to.

The guy grabbed Jack by the throat and pressed the tip of the blade against his cheek, dangerously close to his eye.

"Now, you're going to tell me where you came from, and you're going to let us take your shit. And if I feel generous enough, I'll leave you with one intact eye before I let you go."

The tip of the blade dug into Jack's skin. He felt something warm running down his cheek. He couldn't tell these people about the farm. If he did, they would go there, and they would find Linda. They would surely kill her before pillaging his home. And then again, if he died, Linda would be left to fend for herself. Would that be any better than leading them there?

"Wait, Oliver. I recognize him," the tall guy said.

The blade instantly stopped pressing against Jack as the young guy, Oliver, turned around to look at his companion. All eyes were now fixed on the bearded man.

"He's the farm boy," the man said. "The one who worked in the antique shop."

Oliver turned to face Jack again, a grin plastered on his face.

"Oh, that's right," he said. "He's married to that hot chick from the phone company. Where is she now, by the way? I always fantasized about fucking her, but, you know, laws and all that. But now that there ain't nobody to stop me, I think I might introduce myself to her."

"Don't you fucking touch her!" Jack jerked forward, causing the captor to recoil a step back. His companions roared in laughter. Oliver looked like he just got slapped, but then he smiled again. "Oh, I see. Where is she now? She still back at that farm of yours?"

Jack tugged at the restrains, no longer caring about the burning in his wrists. He wanted to rip this teenager apart, wipe that ugly grin off his face with the bottom of his boot.

"You know how to get to that farm, Clive?" Oliver asked the bearded guy.

"Yup. Lorraine and I drove past his farm once before the shit. Nice place. Probably full of supplies," the bearded guy said.

"I don't like farms," Oliver said. "And I don't like this asshole thinking he's better than us because he has his own property, isolating himself and shit. Let's burn the place down after we're done with it."

"I'm staying here," the bearded guy said. "Somebody's gotta keep watch on the farmer."

"Yeah. Come on, Lorraine," Oliver said.

The bearded guy pushed himself away from the door and opened it. Oliver looked at Jack and winked. "I'll be sure to tell your wife you're thinking about her," he said and exited through the door.

Jack growled and tugged at the restrains again. He sounded like one of those infected as he fought to free himself. All three captors were out, and the doors were closed, leaving Jack alone with the silence in the cold room. Jack inhaled a deep breath and screamed at the top of his lungs. He tugged his hands until his wrists started to burn. It could have been one minute or one hour, he had no idea, but by the time he was done, he was entirely drained.

Anger had subsided, and new thoughts punctuated his mind instead. What was going to happen to Linda? What were they going to do when they found her? Did she even remain in her room? If she did, then they might not even run into her. No, she wasn't in the room. He saw her silhouette in the window when he left.

Tears blurred his vision. They were going to kill her, and then they were going to kill him. There was a silver lining in this whole thing. It would finally be over. He and Linda would be reunited in the afterlife, he was sure of it. Maybe that's where she already was, waiting for him, and what remained of her on this earth was just the walking corpse, who he tried to maintain a fragment of a normal life with.

Jack took deep breaths, calmed down, and then felt with his fingers what his hands were tied with. His fingers ran across the unmistakably smooth surface of the duct tape. He had to cut through the tape. He looked around the room, and saw a metal pipe leaning on the wall to his left. Not good enough to cut through the tape, though, and even if it was, he wouldn't be able to reach it without falling and alerting the guard outside.

He still had his wristwatch on. He wouldn't have noticed it if part of his watch hadn't snagged the edge of the tape. He had no choice but to try and free himself using his watch. He coiled his wrists in steady motions, the watch skipping against the tape. He wasn't sure what was going on exactly over there, he was just trying to cut through the tape somehow.

After what must have felt like a hundred wiggles of his wrists, the watch caught a part of the tape firmly. Jack violently moved his wrists down and felt part of the tape ripping. He was still bound firmly, but it was a start. He repeated the motion, and felt the second layer tearing, and then the third one. With each tear, he could wiggle his wrists more.

Jack was overcome by a sense euphoria. Escape was close, he could feel it. When the tape was torn enough, Jack moved his hands in opposite directions to widen the tear. Although he had to use a lot of his strength, he was succeeding. Little by little, the tear was widening, until his wrists tugged free.

Jack huffed in excitement and triumph as he hastily unstuck the rest of the tape from his skin. His wrists cried out in both pain and relief. With his newfound freedom, Jack tip-toed to the pipe on the floor and picked it up. It was heavy, and Jack hoped that he'd be able to take a good swing at the tall guy before he shot at him.

He gripped the pipe with both hands, stood with his back against the wall next to the door, and shouted, "Hey! Hey, you! I need help!"

He waited. There was no response. For all he knew, the guy changed his mind and left with his companions.

"Come on, man! I just wanna talk!" Jack shouted.

More silence ensued. Jack was tempted to open the door and step outside. He was sure that they hadn't locked it. But then he heard the faint sound of footsteps approaching. Jack gripped the bar so hard that his knuckles turned white. He was ready. He would attack as soon as the door opened. Then, he would run back to his truck and drive to the farm. Then, he would kill the other two. He just hoped that he wouldn't be too late. They already had a good head start on him.

The knob turned, and the door opened inward. Jack swung the pipe over his shoulder. The bearded guy stepped inside, his reticent stare turning into a wide-eyed expression of horror. By the time he saw Jack in his peripheral vision, it was already too late.

Jack brought the pipe down. It connected with the guy's skull with a dull *bonk*. The impact was so strong that Jack felt the vibration going like a shockwave all the way to his wrists. The man didn't even yelp. He dropped his rifle and fell sideways. He was dead, Jack was sure of it.

But then the man grabbed at his head, groaning in pain. Blood trickled between his fingers and dripped onto the floor. Jack dropped the pipe, causing it to clang on the floor, while he bent down to pick up the assault rifle. As soon as it was in his hands, he flicked the safety off and pointed it at the man.

"No, no, wait! Please!" the bearded man's eyes widened and he raised one palm toward Jack, his fingers violently trembling. "I can help you. We can go there together and I'll tell them to leave! We'll go back to town and we won't touch you again!"

Jack gritted his teeth. He kept the man's head in the crosshairs of the firearm.

"You'd retaliate," Jack said as he squeezed the trigger.

The man didn't even have time to beg Jack before the bullet went through his eye and painted the wall behind him red. The dead body of the bearded man slumped sideways, his remaining eye wide in shock, his mouth agape, while blood pooled around his head.

Fuck that guy. Fuck all of them for killing the people who were trying to survive. Jack spat on his corpse and walked through the door, his finger on the trigger and ready to shoot anyone in his way.

It was time to rescue Linda.

Chapter Thirteen

The thought of dying was seen in an entirely different light now. It was no longer the fear of dying and going into the afterlife. It was the fear of dying and leaving the most cherished person in the world behind.

"Okay, let's see where we stopped with the story," Linda said as she slithered deeper under the covers and grabbed *The Witch of the Woods* from the nightstand.

The candlelight on the nightstand that dimly illuminated the bedroom cast shadows on Linda's face. Jack had suggested that he use a flashlight to illuminate the book for her, but Linda shook her head, stating that they needed to preserve the batteries, if possible.

Linda opened the book on the familiar page that had an illustration of the two children protagonists, Will and Zara, standing in front of an old woman draped in a cloak.

"I gotta get you a new book," Jack said with a head shake.

"No, I like this one," Linda said. "It's a nice story about love."

"The main characters are kids. I think they're just friends."

"Friends or not, it's still a kind of love. If you're not interested, I can just read silently." Linda shot Jack a contemptuous glare.

"No, no. I'm interested. Can't wait to see what happens next," Jack joked as he scooted closer to Linda.

Linda gave him a brusque smile, and then turned to the book before clearing her throat.

"The Witch offered to help Will and Zara find a way back. "I can help you," she said. "But you have to give me something in return." Zara asked Will to go because she knew how dangerous the Witch was, "We'll find our own way back, thank you," she said, much to the Witch's anger. But the witch warned them of the dangers in the forest. "Scary things come out at night and eat children, especially the ones as cute as you," she said. Zara and Will froze. The woods grew darker with each passing second. "We'll give you want you want, just help us get back home," Will said. The Witch smiled in satisfaction. "I want your soul."

Linda turned to the next page. This one illustrated the witch grinning madly under a crooked nose, holding a glowing white ball in her hand. The boy had a blank stare in his eye, his shoulders drooped, and the girl looked at the boy in a concerned manner. Linda continued reading.

"The children thought for a moment. They knew that didn't have a lot of time. Without hesitation, Will agreed to surrender his soul to the Witch. "Splendid!" The Witch danced with a maniacal cackle. She told Will to put out his hand, and when the hag touched him, he felt something happening. The Witch pulled her hand back and had a bright ball in her palm – Will's soul. "Very well, I will show you how to get home," The Witch said, pointing a crooked finger in one direction while not taking her eyes off Will's soul."

The next page showed Will and Zara sitting on swings, but Will had the same, stupefied stare in his eye, as if he hadn't slept for days. Zara's gaze was focused on him in a look that expressed worry.

"Are we sure this story is for children?" Jack sardonically asked.

Linda snuggled up to him. She gave Jack a peck on the forehead and turned her head back to the book.

"True to her word, the Witch showed them the right way home. Zara rejoiced, but Will didn't seem to care. In fact, it soon became clear that Will was not the same boy that Zara knew. He no longer seemed to enjoy when the two of them played. He rarely looked at Zara. He never laughed. The Witch had led them home, but at a heavy cost. Zara wanted her friend back. She could not be happy as long as he was not happy."

Linda closed the book all of a sudden.

"What? No more reading tonight?" Jack asked.

Linda placed the book on the nightstand and blew out the candle. The room plunged into darkness immediately. Linda turned to Jack and snuggled up to him again. "I'm a little tired tonight," she said as she placed her head on his chest.

Jack gently ran his fingers down her shoulder. She suddenly felt cold, so he pulled the blanket up to cover her. She didn't respond to the gesture.

"Something bothering you, babe?" Jack asked. "The story gets better, you know?

"I want to talk about something," Linda said.

She looked concerned, and Jack knew that the talk they were about to have was going to be serious. Jack raised his head to look at her. He could only see the top of her head from here, but even if she were turned toward him, it would be too dark to see her face.

"What's wrong, Lin?" Jack asked as he brushed the hair out of her face and behind her ear.

He heard Linda gulping. She moved her head up so that she was facing him and said, "If I ever… if I get infec–"

"No. Linda, we talked about this before, and I refuse to–"

"Jack, listen to me," Linda said as she stood up and distanced herself from him. "Please."

He was about to interrupt her until she said "please." She sounded fragile when she said that, and he had no choice but to comply.

"Okay. Okay, Linda," Jack said, realizing how serious she was about this.

"If I ever get infected, I need you to promise me that… promise me that you'll kill me," her voice cracked toward the end.

Jack put a hand on her cheek and tried to reel her in, but she resisted.

"Promise me, Jack," she said sternly.

"Linda, you know I can't promise that."

"Promise me!" she raised her voice and sniffled as she firmly put her hands on Jack's cheeks.

She wasn't going to let this go until she heard the answer that she wanted to hear. Jack paused. For a moment, the image of Linda shambling like a zombie went through his head. He felt his hands and feet becoming cold at that thought.

"If you ever get bitten, then I'll let you bite me, and then we'll be together in undeath," Jack said.

"Jack, please don't joke about these things," Linda said.

"I'm not. Look, what do you want me to say, Linda? That I'll shoot you in the head if you become like one of them? Because I'll tell you right away, that's not happening. I am never going to–"

"Jack. Please," Linda said, calmly this time, her voice making her sound defeated.

That's when Jack realized how serious she really was about this. It wasn't just some philosophical and hypothetical topic to discuss. No, this was something that might become a reality in the not-so-distant future.

Even tomorrow, a voice inside Jack's head said, further causing his panic to exacerbate.

"Please, Jack," Linda repeated. "Promise me."

"Okay, Linda. Alright. I promise," Jack said.

Linda remained stiff for a moment, and then relaxed and leaned her head on Jack's chest. She was shuddering, and Jack consoled her by stroking her back and wiping her tears.

He hoped that Linda hadn't figured out that he was lying.

Chapter Fourteen

"Step on it!" Oliver commanded Lorraine.

"Do you wanna drive, fuckface?" Lorraine retorted.

The car trundled on the cracked, pothole-riddled road. Oliver was in the passenger seat, holding his gun in his lap and wiping it with a dirty rag. The grease only transferred from the rag onto the gun. When he looked up, he saw the annoying green landscapes stretching on both sides of the road.

"I fuckin' hate the nature," he said, squinting, even though the sun was obscured by the clouds.

"Why? I think it's kinda nice," Lorraine said. "I don't see why we shouldn't claim the farm for our own."

"Because it's a fucking farm!" Oliver retorted. "Who would wanna be in the middle of fuckin' nowhere, surrounded by cow shit and smelling like shit all day long?"

"You already smell like shit, so you're halfway there."

"Fuck you."

Even before everything went down with the biters, Oliver wasn't taking care of his personal hygiene much. He never had the chance for it because he was homeless. When he was sixteen, his parents kicked him out of the house when they found out that he was molesting his little sister, and he'd been living on the streets since then.

When the outbreak started, Oliver saw an opportunity, so he took it. He had already killed once by then, so doing it again was not a problem for him. He found guns, he made friends with people who accepted him as their own, and his life had never been better. For most people, the outbreak was a nightmare. For Oliver, it was a rescue.

Not only did he have a home now, but he could finally live how he always wanted to – without worrying about the consequences. Stealing, murdering, raping… those things exhilarated him beyond words.

Even as he sat in the car and eagerly awaited to reach the farm, he already got excited at the thought of finding the farmer's wife inside the house. He was going to have a lot of fun with her before killing her.

"There it is," Lorraine said.

Oliver looked up. Down the dirt road was a lonesome, fenced-off house. Oliver couldn't help but become angry. That son of a bitch farmer thought he was better than everyone, buying a farm for himself away from the town and making it so well defended. What a prick. Oliver was going to teach him a lesson. After finishing his wife off, he would cut off her head, burn the farm, and bring the head back to the farmer to show it to him before killing him.

The car drove across the grass, ignoring the one undead who roamed it, and stopped a few feet from the property's fence. Lorraine and Oliver got out of the car. The fence had a padlock, but that was not a problem. Oliver retrieved the bolt cutter from the trunk and approached the fence. The cutter's blade snapped through the links effortlessly, causing the padlock to slump on the ground with a rattle along with the chain.

"Honey! I'm home!" Oliver said perkily as he opened the gate.

Upon exiting the room where they kept him imprisoned, Jack realized that he was in a large warehouse of some sort. He kept his guard up because he knew that the people who had heard the gunshot would be here soon to investigate.

Sure enough, loud footsteps came thundering from somewhere a moment later. Jack held the assault rifle trained in front of him. He had already used it before on a shooting range, so he was familiar with its weight, recoil, and every other mechanic that came with it.

Two men ran from around the corner. The one in front didn't even see Jack before the bullets rained on him. The other one managed to duck behind a shipment container before Jack could shoot him.

The man peeked out a moment later, pointing a gun at Jack. Jack jumped to the right behind cover just as a loud gunshot filled the air. He heard the bullets grazing the corner of the boxes that he ran behind, missing him by mere inches.

"I'll kill you for that, you motherfucker!" the guy shouted.

More gunshots ensued, and Jack knew that he had two choices – either wait until the attacker was out of ammo, or try to get the drop on him from a different position. He opted for the latter.

He walked alongside the wall and skirted between the abandoned, dusty boxes and containers, listening to the gunshots echoing in the enormous warehouse. The attacker thought that Jack was still behind the same cover, which gave Jack the advantage. He stepped out from the corner and faced the assailant from behind. The man still had no idea that Jack was behind him.

Jack held the rifle pointed at the man and slowly walked toward him. He didn't need to be quiet because the gunshots had muffled his footsteps. The attacker kept peeking and firing an occasional bullet. When Jack was finally close enough to the assailant, he gently prodded him with the barrel of the gun.

The man froze. Jack didn't want him to surrender. He wanted him to know that he had lost, and to feel the fear that this person probably made other people feel when he hunted them like they were animals. Before the attacker could even start pleading, Jack pointed the rifle to the back of the guy's head and fired a bullet. The man shot forward and slammed against the ground, blood immediately spreading in a wide pool on the floor around his face.

"You're not stopping me from saving my wife," Jack said, anger swirling inside him.

He ran toward the door that looked like it might lead outside. As soon as he burst through the door, daylight blinded him. The undead were at the fence past the warehouse yard, clawing and trying to reach Jack. He knew exactly where he was. His truck was only a few blocks away.

Jack fired bullets into the heads of the undead that blocked his way, then opened the gate and bolted down the street toward his truck. He hoped to God not to run into any more of those people who caught him.

The undead were congregating toward the warehouse, the gunshots summoning them like dinner bells. Jack sprinted past them, ignoring them as much as he could, and shooting only the ones that were in his way.

One of them grabbed him by the sleeve, but Jack managed to tear out of his bony grip.

He prayed that his truck was still there and intact. Luck would have it that it was exactly how he had left it. He didn't even care about losing his revolver and backpack. He had the rifle and that would help him against the thugs. He practically jumped into the truck, started it, and floored the gas pedal.

****

Oliver could hardly wait to see what he would find inside the house. The front door was locked, so he broke the window by throwing the bolt cutters through it, much to the grumbling of Lorraine. He climbed inside, careful not to snag his jacket on any of the jutting shards. Lorraine followed him inside, her gun drawn, her face conveying caution.

"Helloooo? Anybody hoooome?" Oliver called out in a sing-song voice.

A sound came from upstairs. The wife was here. Lorraine looked at Oliver and shrugged. "I'll go check it out," she said.

"Don't go hurting the woman, you hear? It's not the same if they don't scream."

Lorraine ignored his remark and climbed the stairs, the gun pointed at the top of the staircase. Oliver went to check the rest of the ground floor. The house was really nice, he noticed. He couldn't help but feel a pang of envy toward the farmer. He had it all – lots of money, a big house, and a beautiful wife.

That angered Oliver. It made him feel like a failure. In the quiet moments, he always dreamed about living in his own house or apartment with a beautiful wife and children, but the insatiable desire for breaking the rules always got in the way. The farmer was an accomplished man – until today. After today, he would be just another victim in the outbreak.

As Oliver walked past the living room, he made sure to knock things over and make a mess. Vases broke on the floor, the bookshelf toppled, the TV's screen broke. He went to the kitchen and opened the pantry. Oliver felt like he had won a lottery. His mouth stretched into a grin as he entered and darted his eyes at the abundance of food that the farmer had stockpiled.

There was enough here to keep Oliver fed for at least two months, and maybe even more. He didn't have a backpack on him, so he began putting cans in his pockets. He would unload them into the car, and then come back for the rest. He would need to make at least four trips he reckoned, but he didn't mind.

"Boy, oh boy. There's gonna be good eatings tonight!" he said to himself complacently.

A gunshot came from upstairs, startling Oliver and almost causing him to drop the can of baked beans. The shot was followed by a thud, then scratching, shuffling, and finally, silence. Oliver instinctively looked up, as if he could see through the ceiling.

"Lorraine, you good?" he asked.

More shuffling ensued, but Lorraine didn't respond.

"Lorraine!" Oliver repeated.

Frustrated that she couldn't hear him, Oliver slammed the can in his hand on the ground and strode to the stairs. He stomped upstairs, ready to give Lorraine a piece of his mind.

"Hey! Are you fucking deaf or so–"

His throat caught his words when he saw feet splayed on the floor, peeking out of a room on the left. The shoes belonged to Lorraine. Oliver took out his pistol and pointed it down the corridor, the indignance suddenly gone and replaced by a sense of apprehension.

"Lorraine?" Oliver said as he approached the room where Lorraine was.

She was on her back, a chunk of her throat missing, blood trickling out of her open mouth. Her eyes stared vacantly at the ceiling. The front of her jacket was drenched in blood. Oliver looked into the room, his hands now shaking.

He couldn't shake the feeling that coming here was a big mistake. Suddenly, he wanted nothing more than to get out of here. Who cares about the farm and the wife, anyway? He would take the supplies that he put in his pockets and leave. He would need to leave Lorraine here, but she was dead, anyway. It was her fault for not being careful enough.

Oliver turned to go back to the stairs and saw a figure covered in fresh blood standing in front of him. He raised his gun just as the woman lunged at him.

Gunshots filled the air.

****

Jack had bumped into a few undead on his way back to the farm. He was driving dangerously fast, and he didn't care. He needed to get back home as soon as possible – that's all that mattered.

"Come on, dammit. Come on!" he shouted at the truck, trying to force it to go faster.

The engine roared so loudly that Jack expected it to attract every undead in the state. The farm came into view much faster than it was supposed to, even though Jack felt as though he was far too late. A car was parked in front of the fence.

Shit. Shit. Shit!

He stepped on the brakes too late. The truck slid across the grass and bumped into the back of the car parked in front. The crash wasn't horrible, but it was strong enough to cause Jack to lurch forward. The bang probably alerted the intruders, too.

Jack grabbed the rifle and ran out of the truck. He didn't care about being reckless. The fence was open and the window of the living room broken. Panic surged through him at the thought of those two finding Linda and putting a bullet in her head. Jack pointed the gun through the window and scanned the living room, already winded. He hadn't bothered unlocking the front door. He jumped through the window, and once more scanned the living room.

The place was in disarray. It looked as if the house had suffered a massive earthquake. Jack took a step toward the kitchen before he heard a soft sound upstairs.

"Linda!" Jack shouted and ran upstairs.

As soon as he reached the top of the staircase, he pointed the gun down the corridor, his finger on the trigger. He almost pulled it, but then his brain registered what his eyes were seeing, like a laggy internet connection on a video call.

Linda was on all fours, her teeth buried in the face of one of the attackers. Jack immediately recognized the victim as the young guy who had threatened Jack. He was on his back, his arms spread as if he was crucified. His upper lip was missing all the way to the nose, revealing his crooked teeth. His left eye was a mushy socket, and his neck was missing a chunk of flesh and cartilage all the way to the backbone.

Jack would have been happy to see the fucker dead in any other situation, but right then, he was nothing short of relieved to see Linda was okay. He screamed in restfulness and dropped on his knees next to Linda.

"Linda! Baby, are you alright?! Did they hurt you?!" Tears welled up in his eyes as he put a hand on her back. "I never should have left you, I'm so sorry, Linda."

Linda didn't acknowledge Jack's presence. She feasted on the dead body of her victim. Jack stroked her back, and then felt something cold and wet on his fingers. He pulled his hand back and saw blood.

When he looked at Linda, he saw four red spots on her back. He ran to the other side and noticed red splotches there, too. The son of a bitch must have shot her. That caused Jack's panic to further swell, but it soon became apparent that Linda was completely okay and unfazed by the gunshot wounds. That both worried him and gave him a sense of relief.

Jack looked up and saw someone's feet peeking from Linda's room. He stood up and rushed to the door. It was the woman who accompanied the young guy to the house. She, too, was dead. Good riddance.

Jack looked at his wife. She pulled her head back and snapped off the corpse's lower lip like it was a piece of cheese.

"I am never going to leave you again, Linda. I promise," he said. "I'll find a way to keep you fed and to have us survive, but I am not going to put you in danger again. I love you, Linda."

Although she didn't respond, she continued eating, and in a strange way, Jack felt like that was her way of reciprocating the emotions.

Chapter Fifteen

The world was on fire. It was impossible to tell if they would even wake up to see the next daylight. And yet whenever he looked at her, and she smiled at him, he somehow knew that everything was going to be okay.

"Jack! Jack, wake up!" Linda's shaking startled Jack awake.

He sat ramrod straight in bed, his mind boggled.

"What's wrong?" Jack asked with a slurred speech.

"Something's happening downstairs!" Linda said in a panicked whisper.

That's when he heard it. Something clattered downstairs. Jack stood up and put his jeans on. Linda mimicked his gesture and started putting her clothes on, too.

"No, you stay here," Jack said as he buckled his jeans. "I'll go and check it out."

"Nolan and the others could be in trouble. We have to hurry," Linda said.

Jack regretted forgetting his firearms downstairs, especially now when he had guests in the house. So stupid of him to forget such an important thing! Jack turned the knob and gently opened the door.

It produced a low creak, but in the absence of any other noise, it sounded like a trumpet. Jack peeked toward the stairs. A dull thud resounded somewhere, followed by hushed, hasty voices. What was going on down there?

Jack stepped outside, walking on his toes as he approached the top of the stairs.

Shuffling noises became prominent. He also heard a deep voice saying something, but he couldn't make out the words. He thought that the voice belonged to Chris. Jack descended the stairs, step by step, keeping his eyes fixated on the living room. Another clamor caused him to pause.

"Watch it!" the voice said.

It was definitely Chris. Feeling just a tiny bit relieved, Jack continued descending. Once he reached the bottom, he peeked toward the source of the sound. A bulky figure stood in front of the cupboard next to the TV, rummaging through one of the drawers. Behind the bulky figure was a tiny one that without a doubt belonged to Nathan.

Sensing Jack's presence, Nathan turned around. Even in the darkness of the room, Jack saw the boy's eyes widening. Chris continued rummaging and stuffing things into a bag, unaware of what was going on. He then closed the drawer and spun around, then froze. For a moment, neither Jack nor Chris spoke.

"Jack. Uh... I was looking for uh..." Chris started, but obviously was at a loss for words.

"What's going on here? You trying to rob us?" Jack asked.

Linda walked up behind Jack. He silently swore because she didn't stay in the bedroom. Just then, another figure walked in through the front door. When Nolan saw the commotion in the living room, his jaw dropped, similarly to Chris' reaction.

"What are you guys doing?" Jack asked, his eyes gravitating to the bag in Chris' hand.

Chris grabbed something long that stood by the wall and pointed it at Jack. Jack recoiled when he realized that it was his rifle.

"I'm sorry that it had to come to this, man," Chris said. "We don't wanna do this, but you leave us no choice."

"Chris, put the gun down, dammit!" Nolan commanded. "Nathan, get over here. Now."

The kid ran up to his father. Nolan raised a palm toward Jack and said, "Folks, we are really sorry about it, alright? We'll just be taking your car and a little bit of your food. Nobody's gonna get hurt, okay?"

"And the rifle," Chris exclaimed. "You're lucky we're good people and decided not to take everything y'all have."

"We saved you from those infected, you asshole!" Jack snapped as he took a step forward.

In that moment, he wanted to punch Chris in the face. How dare he repay their hospitality like this?

"Stay back, motherfucker!" Chris pointed the gun at Jack, clutching it more firmly.

That caused Jack to freeze in his tracks. He was fuming. Linda stopped next to Jack and said, "Look, just take what you want and leave. We don't want any trouble, okay?"

"Chris, come on. Leave the rifle," Nolan said. "The gate's already open and the keys are in the car. If we don't hurry, the undead will swarm this place soon."

Chris briefly looked at Nolan, and then at Jack. "No, I'm keeping the rifle. We need protection," he said. "Also, your watch. I want it."

"No fucking way," Jack shook his head.

"That wasn't a request," Chris hissed.

Voices broke out, people trying to calm down Chris and Jack. In that moment of heat, Chris lowered his gun and looked in Nolan's direction as he shouted. This was Jack's opportunity. He bull-rushed and tackled Chris before the oaf could even see what was going on.

Wrestling ensued as the two fought over the rifle while voices in the room shouted at them. Jack was only vaguely aware of them. He was going to wrestle the gun away from this motherfucker, and then he was going to strip him naked and kick all three of them off his property.

He barely had time to entertain that thought before a loud bang filled the air, silencing the voices in the room and freezing everyone – everyone except Jack. Jack's ears rung, but he ignored the deafening noise. He punched Chris in the face, and the man's grip on the rifle loosened. Jack yanked the rifle away and stood up, a triumphant smile on his face. Chris raised his palms in surrender.

"J-Jack?" a small voice behind him said, and that caused the anger to hiss out of him like air from a sealed bag.

Jack turned around. Linda stood in the middle of the room, staring down. A red splotch appeared on her stomach. She looked at Jack with eyes wide and mouth agape. The moment seemed to freeze.

And then Linda fell.

Chapter Sixteen

In the following days after escaping the warehouse, Jack expected retaliation from the people in Eugene. He couldn't be sure if the group that had attacked him was as small as they looked or if they were well organized with dozens and hundreds of people patrolling the town. The warehouse that he had been brought to and beaten up, although spacious, was almost entirely empty, which told Jack that he might have overestimated the group's power.

Still, he kept a lookout through his window to make sure no cars would be pulling up. Something good came out of his visit to Eugene, too. He had lost his revolver, but he got new weapons from the scavengers. He also got their car, which he decided to park behind the house and cover with a rain sheet. He would have just left it outside, but he didn't want to draw any attention, especially not attention from people who might either recognize the vehicle as one belonging to their friends, or as an opportunity for escape.

The most important thing that Jack managed to get was food for Linda. There were two whole bodies in his house, and Linda incessantly munched on them without a moment of break. Jack used that moment of Linda's distraction to restrain her and put her back in the room again. He dragged the two corpses into the room and left them within Linda's reach.

Later that night when he walked in, both bodies were eaten beyond recognition. There was still a lot of meat on them, and some of the organs were intact, but

Linda was quickly consuming what little remained on their bones.

The smell was unbearable by then. Jack gagged, feeling the meager lunch climbing up his throat in the form of bile. He suppressed it, and took a moment to allow his nose to adjust to the redolence in the room. He then opened the window behind Linda and left the door open to vent the bad air.

After inspecting Linda's bullet wounds, he deduced that she, indeed, wasn't bothered by them, so he decided not to do anything to patch her up. The bullets had exited her body anyway, which he later found out when he saw them lodged in the ceiling and the wall in the corridor.

Jack continued reading *The Witch of the Woods* to Linda while she ate. In the story, Zara went back to the woods alone to get Will's soul from the Witch. The Witch told Zara that she could have Will's soul in exchange for the girl's. But Zara had already come prepared. She knew that the Witch would try to trick her into giving her the soul, so she devised a trick.

She told the Witch that there was a secret place where many children gathered and played every day, and that she could have all their souls if she gave her back Will's. The Witch, thirsty for the children's souls, eagerly returned Will's soul to Zara and demanded to be taken to that secret place.

Zara led her to the edge of a cliff and pushed her off. The Witch plummeted to the rocky bottom and died. Zara then went into the Witch's cabin and collected all the souls of the other unfortunate children and released them to return to their owners. She returned the soul to Will and he immediately became his old self again.

With the Witch gone, the children spent many, many days playing in the woods.

"What do you think?" Jack closed the book with a thud and looked at Linda to gauge her reaction. She was still eating. Nothing unexpected. Jack never understood why Linda liked this story so much. Now that she was undead, his indifference toward *The Witch of the Woods* morphed into hate.

He was angry at the story, but at the same time, a profound sense of sadness overcame him. Will and Zara had a happy ending, and Jack hated them for that. He was jealous, and he wanted nothing more than to have a happy ending with Linda.

Maybe that's what Linda was trying to tell him this whole time – that if Jack ever were to lose his soul, or in this case get infected, she would find a way to bring him back. For a moment, he wondered what it would be like if the tables were turned, and he was the one who got infected, and not her.

Linda firmly believed that getting infected was the end of all things. Although Jack never explicitly told her that he wanted her to shoot him in case he got infected, she said that she would do so, but she also said that she would most likely end up shooting herself afterwards, too.

Whenever they did discuss the infection, it was one-sided in a way that they discussed what Jack should do to Linda in case she got bitten. Jack had promised her that he would end her if that happened. Now, as he watched her eating the dead body of another human, reduced to everything she feared becoming, Jack's cheeks burned with shame and newfound pain that he couldn't describe. He leaned forward, staring at Linda's bullet-riddled back.

"I know I promised, Lin. I know," he said. "But… I can't do it." His eyes warmed up as he felt the tears forming in them. "I promised you, but… I can't let you go. I love you too much. If you die, then I'll die with you. I also said that I would let you bite me if that ever happened. Maybe… maybe that's the solution."

Jack stood up from the chair dazed, and approached Linda with slow steps. He got on his knees next to her. He was so close that he could now see the dry and pale skin on her face cracking and flaking off. The smell of death was so strong that Jack felt like he was going to pass out. Droplets of blood flew in every direction as Linda took a bite of the dead woman's arm, but the disgusting details didn't faze Jack.

He raised one hand and reached toward her face. She didn't seem to notice. He yearned for her touch, no matter how cold or corpse-like it felt. He needed to feel her to know that she was still here, still real. Jack's finger brushed Linda's ear. She felt ice-cold to the touch, the skin surprisingly smooth.

Becoming more daring, Jack brushed Linda's hair behind her ear and then caressed her cheek with the backs of his fingers. Linda didn't so much as glance in his direction. Jack leaned toward her, suddenly overcome by an insatiable desire to be close to his wife. He didn't care that she hadn't bathed in months and smelled like hot garbage. He didn't care that she had old and fresh blood all over her. He didn't care that her hair was disheveled and looked like dry hay.

She was still his wife, and she was as attractive as the day he met her. Jack's lips brushed against Linda's ear, and he felt his breath quavering like it did when they first kissed when they went rafting. Jack kissed Linda on the cheek. His lips turned cold, but his body burned with an intensity that he hadn't known in a long time. He pressed his cheek against hers and closed his eyes.

He strongly wanted to grab Linda by the cheeks and kiss her on the lips, not caring if she would bite his tongue off. It felt so easy to just give into that feeling of surrendering entirely to Linda. Before he could entertain that thought, Linda jerked her head toward him and hissed.

Jack jumped backward and screamed, his body acting on instinct as he landed on his rear and scooted away from Linda until his back hit the wall. Linda had already continued eating by then. Jack's vision became blurry from the tears, and he felt like he could no longer suppress them.

He gasped uncontrollably and his shoulders shuddered. Jack buried his face in his hands and sobbed, allowing the floodgates that had been closed for so long to open. Wave after wave flooded in, seemingly endless, but Jack didn't care. He was completely and utterly broken.

He wanted to be able to lay his head on Linda's chest while she consoled him. He wanted to see the smile that she gave him whenever he did something clumsy. He wanted to hear her laugh. He wanted to hear her speaking about the boring stuff that happened at work. He wanted to wake up earlier and see her sleeping in bed next to him.

He just wanted his wife back.

Chapter Seventeen

There is only one thing more horrifying than watching the person you love with your entire existence slipping away, and being unable to do anything to stop it – remembering the happy times of the past and thinking about the future you would never share.

"Linda!" Jack shouted, dropping the rifle and rushing to his wife.

His heart thudded up to his throat and the horrible realization of what had happened dawned on him. He took Linda into his arms and raised her head.

"Linda, baby. Hold on, hold on, you're going to be okay, hold on…" Jack muttered as he pressed against the wound on her abdomen.

Almost immediately, warm blood enveloped his palm and fingers.

"What the fuck, Chris?!" Jack heard Nolan's voice through a tunnel.

"No time for that, Nolan! Come on, they're already here!" Chris shouted.

Accompanied by the shouts came the deafening moans of the undead. Jack hadn't even bothered to look toward the door. He was solely focused on Linda. Her chest heaved up and down in violent motions, and she looked unable to breathe in properly. She then coughed, and a trickle of blood ran out of her mouth and slid toward her ear.

She wasn't going to make it, Jack knew that. She needed a doctor, but there wasn't one anywhere close by.

The closest ambulance was in Eugene, and Eugene was a goddamn mess.

Linda's mouth contorted into various shapes as she tried to say something, but Jack couldn't hear her over the sound of the car's engine outside. He looked at the entrance and saw the headlights illuminating a shambling undead walking toward the house, arms outstretched toward Jack.

Linda's car lurched forward and bumped into the undead, causing him to fall like a ragdoll. The car's engine screeched as the vehicle went outside the property, violently slamming the fence in the process, before gaining speed and leaving the farm behind in dust.

The undead were approaching the defenseless farm, and Jack had to do something. He looked at Linda. Her eyes fluttered, and her breathing became wheezy. Jack had an idea, and he wasn't sure if he'd even call it an idea. He opened the wardrobe and grabbed his revolver.

He then took a handful of bullets and with the revolver, stepped outside. He shot the undead who got hit by the car, and then another one who had just walked through the fence. The next one who came through was a middle-aged man in torn clothes.

"Come on, in here!" Jack called to him, refusing to shoot him.

The undead was slow, but Jack made the mistake of being careless in the spur of the moment. His heel caught on one of the porch steps and he fell backward, slamming his head against the floor. Stars flew across his vision, and the undead threw itself upon him.

Jack instinctively put his hands in front of him, managing to stop the man's teeth just inches from his neck. He pushed, but the man was strong. His teeth gnashed with snapping sounds before Jack managed to push him off.

He quickly stood up and got inside the house. The undead followed, and so did the five others who were now close to the fence.

"Come on, you fucker!" Jack taunted him, leading him deeper into the living room.

The undead bumped into the coffee table and knocked over an empty cup. Jack looked back to see Linda on the ground, her head turned to face him, her eyes wide with terror. Jack stepped around her. Linda looked at him, and then at the undead whose eyes had now shifted to Linda.

"Baby, trust me on this. This is going to be over soon, and then you'll be okay, I promise!" Jack cried.

Linda turned her head to the undead and feebly raised her hands as it approached her. The undead fell on top of her and broke through her meager defense with ease. Almost as soon as he fell on top of her, he bit her neck. Linda screamed. She suddenly got a burst of energy that wasn't there before as her legs and arms thrashed against the attacker.

Jack cried as he watched blood coming out of his wife's neck. That was it. One bite was enough. Jack pointed the gun at the undead and shot him in the head. He fell limply on top of Linda, and by then, the other undead were walking inside. Jack shot them all one by one, the gunshots reverberating in the house, the attackers falling one by one, until the only sound that remained was Jack's heavy panting.

He had to get back to Linda. He had to hold her hand and tell her that everything was going to be okay as she transitioned to her new form. Jack dropped the revolver, ran to his wife, and rolled the undead off her.

"Linda? Linda, I'm here, baby. I'm here!" Jack chanted as he fell to his knees and grabbed his wife's hand.

She didn't respond.

"Linda?" Jack called out and put a hand on Linda's cheek.

Her eyes were closed, her mouth slightly agape, her face and lips pale. Jack shook her. "Linda. Baby, wake up. Baby, please, wake up. Wake up, wake up, wa–"

His words were interrupted by a crying fit.

Linda was dead.

Chapter Eighteen

Jack had a spare set of padlocks and chains, so he easily replaced the one that was cut at the gate. Cleaning the living room took a little time, and when he was done sweeping the broken shards, it looked a lot emptier than before. The blood in the corridor upstairs took some time, but Jack had nothing better to do anyway.

The biggest problem was the broken window in the living room. Jack had no way of replacing the pane of glass, so instead of doing that, he boarded up the window and pulled the blinds down. The room would be significantly darker, but it was better than having cold air wafting inside.

Linda had finished eating her buffet much sooner than Jack expected, leaving only bones and a little bit of meat. Flies had begun buzzing around the dead bodies, and the rancid smell was causing Jack's eyes to tear up. He had to throw out the mutilated remains.

He hadn't bothered burying them. Fuck them. he put their remains in trash bags and drove them to the woods, where he tossed the bags. He then decided to give Linda a bath. But scrubbing her with a sponge was not possible, of course, so what he did instead was that he brought in a hose and washed her with the stream.

The entire time, Linda hissed and growled at him, trying to reach him, and Jack couldn't tell if it was because she was hungry, or because the hose was angering her. He had adjusted the temperature of the water to how she used to like it, but she still got angry. Once the hose was done and Linda dripping with water, she looked much cleaner. He couldn't help but smile seeing her with wet hair drooping over her face. He loved how she looked after washing her hair.

She still smelled horrible, and Jack couldn't give her a change of clothes, so he settled for this meager bath. He told himself that he would need to get used to the fact that this was what Linda was going to be like now. After cleaning her, Jack threw another chicken to Linda for dinner, reverting to her previous, sloppy and dirty self as soon as she took the first bite.

Jack used that opportunity to hose down the room and clean as much of the crusted blood as he could. Aside from the blood, there were also undigested pieces of meat and locks of Linda's hair. He knew that the room wouldn't stay clean this way for long, but he had to try and keep it as fresh as possible.

The smell still lingered when he was done, but less potently so. Jack thought about changing the mattress as well, but Linda never used the bed, so it wasn't necessary. This room had always been empty. Jack and Linda had kept it empty when they talked about the possibility of having kids one day. Jack had planned on turning the room into a nursery someday. The walls were white, but they could be painted over accordingly, whether the baby turned out to be a boy or a girl.

Remembering that caused another twinge of pain in Jack's heart. He said goodbye to Linda and exited the room before he could become emotional again.

As the days went by, Jack fed the remaining chickens to Linda, leaving the coop empty. He would be lying if he said that it was easy for him to sacrifice the final chicken. Hell, even watching it running around the coop all alone, its friends all dead, and it probably knowing what awaited it, was sad for Jack.

In the end, his wife had to be fed, and there was no going around that.

With all the chickens gone, however, Jack had to think of other ways to feed his wife. The two who came to his farm had dried meat products in their car, but Linda wasn't interested in that. He tossed some jerky in front of her, but she didn't so much as look at it. He waved it in front of her face, but she was unresponsive. He left it on the mattress in case she changed her mind, but when he returned later, the jerky was still there. Now that he thought about it, he didn't even know himself why he thought dry meat products would feed Linda.

He opened his mouth to chide Linda for not eating what he called "quality meat", but then he heard something that caused him to pause. Something that came from the bedroom. He normally wouldn't hear it, but now that sound, or rather the absence of it, caught his attention.

Jack ran out into the corridor and dashed into the bedroom. The sounds immediately became noticeable. It was a voice coming from the radio!

"I know we've been absent for a while, and I am dreadfully sorry to keep you waiting like this, folks!" Gary's jovial voice boomed in the bedroom. "We are now back and we'll be running any tracks you want twenty-four seven, so close your windows, lock your doors, and turn up that volume, because it's gonna be a rough ride."

An old song from the eighties started playing. Jack ran a hand through his hair, his mouth warping into a smile. He laughed loudly, and then clapped his hands together, and then continued laughing. If Gary were in front of him right now, Jack would have kissed him.

He immediately sat on the chair, leaned back, closed his eyes, and listened to the song. Euphoria filled him at the music, and he started to sing along to the lyrics.

He hadn't even realized how much he missed music until he heard it.

When the song ended, Jack felt dread creeping in for the few seconds of silence, but then the next song started playing. Songs played all day long, and as much as Jack wanted to hear Gary speaking, or any other human for that matter, the music worked just as well for him. His mood had been uplifted and remained that way for the rest of the day.

Then in the evening, the song that played stopped halfway through and was replaced by silence. Jack had been sitting in the living room under the candlelight and listening to the music, and when it suddenly stopped, it caused him to jerk his head toward the radio. He stood up, wondering if the batteries had maybe run out. He had a bunch of spares, so that was no problem. As he approached the radio, Gary's familiar voice exploded from the device.

"I hope you folks are staying safe out there. It's been pretty rough for us since we last spoke. The cathedral has been overrun, but not by the infected. It's been overrun by the greedy and selfish people who want to claim Eugene for their own. We lost most of our people in the attack, and we had to find a new sanctuary, but we're now as strong as ever."

Jack sat back down and stared at the radio, listening with rapt attention.

"The government has abandoned us. The army has deserted the checkpoints, leaving the defenseless civilians to die. There are no more rescue missions and evacs being organized. We're on our own, folks."

Jack already knew that at the back of his mind, but having Gary confirm it still made him feel like he wasn't exactly ready to hear that. If Gary's words were true, then it was anarchy out there, no place was safe, and Jack and Linda would have no choice but to stay on the farm.

"We don't need those useless government pricks," Gary said in his perky tone. "Our group is already hard at work organizing a safe haven for you listeners out there. Just hang on a little longer, and we'll have more information soon. Out of obvious reasons, we can't broadcast our location right now, but once our defenses are up, no one will break through, living or dead, unless we allow them to. And then, we can begin rebuilding the world. Together."

That gave Jack a little bit of hope. Survivors were defying the apocalypse. There was a society that wanted to do good for people. But what if it was a trap? What if they were luring people over there just to rob them, or worse?

"I can tell you folks one thing," Gary said. "Don't lose hope. There's way more of you out there than you think. You're not alone."

Gary's speaking stopped and the song from before continued playing, leaving Jack in a deeply pensive state. He knew that realistically speaking, the best chances for survival were with a strong group of people. He couldn't stay on the farm forever. Supplies were dwindling, Eugene was dangerous, and he had Linda to worry about.

But the group of survivors would never accept Jack and Linda. She was undead, the very thing that the survivors were trying to build their defenses against. For a split second, Jack thought about visiting the safe haven alone, just to see what it's like there. They might know something about a cure for this thing. This had to be reversible. It just had to be.

And if it wasn't?

Then Jack would continue living on the farm. He would not abandon Linda just because she was infected.

Chapter Nineteen

Death from heartbreak was real. People from all over the world were known to have died from a broken heart not long after their spouse passed away. It was merciful. Life without the person you loved the most on this earth was not a life at all – at best, it was a life without color – and in death, they would reunite. No pain. No suffering. Just the two of them, together for eternity.

After spending a long time crying over Linda's dead body, Jack collected himself, convinced that she would come back to him. He picked her up, and then gently carried her upstairs. He placed her on the bed of the empty room, gave her a gentle peck on the forehead, and exited.

He spent the entire night cleaning the property. The first thing he did was pile the undead bodies outside the property. He then replaced the chain on the fence – Nolan had cut through the old one – and spent hours cleaning the living room.

He felt numb while scrubbing Linda's blood off the carpet. He couldn't shake the image of her lying on the ground, wheezing, her abdomen bleeding, the zombie taking a bite out of her neck as she thrashed and screamed.

Jack couldn't even remember the last thing she said to him, or the last look she gave him. He was so tired, and so broken, and yet he was on autopilot, cleaning the house, trying to make it impeccable for Linda's return.

She's going to return. I know she is. And when she does, things will be back to the way they were before all this happened, I know it.

Dawn crept into the living room, incessant rays of the sun spearing through the window and blinding Jack. His knees and fingers ached from the scrubbing. The daylight reminded Jack how tired he was. He stood up, ignoring the pang in his lower back, and slumped into the couch.

He was going to take a short nap, that's all. And then he was going to check up on Linda. The undead usually arose within eight hours after dying. Jack closed his eyes, and then he couldn't open them again.

Come back to me, Linda. Come back, baby, he thought to himself as he drifted into a dreamless sleep.

****

He awoke some time later to an incessant scratching noise. He thought that it was something he dreamed about, but when he opened his eyes, the scratching persisted. Jack immediately shot up to his feet, suddenly feeling wide awake as though he had slept ten hours.

Jack ran up the stairs, excitement electrifying him. He stumbled on one of the steps, but managed to stop his face from hitting the floor by planting his palms on the floor. He ran across the corridor, the muscles in his legs burning from exhaustion of working all night long.

"Linda?!" Jack called out just as he stopped in front of the door.

He leaned his ear against the wood, listening attentively. He heard something akin to breathing coming from inside. A smile crept up on his face. Jack gently turned the knob and opened the door. The door produced no sound, even though he somehow expected it to creak.

As he peeked inside, he saw her.

She was standing in front of the bed, facing away from him. *Standing!* Her arms limply dangled by her sides, her head slightly tilted. Low, raspy inhales and exhales escaped her mouth. Jack could hardly contain the happiness he felt in that moment. His plan had worked. The love of his life was back.

"Linda!" Jack opened the door and took a step inside.

Linda shot around and lunged at him without a warning. Jack would have embraced her, but then he saw the look on her face. It was Linda, and yet it wasn't. It felt like staring at a person pretending to be his wife. She stared directly at him, her mouth open, and Jack saw hunger in those eyes.

"Linda, stop! It's me!" he shouted.

He put his hands in front of him and planted one palm on Linda's chest, the other on her forehead. She groaned and growled, her eyes widely focused on his neck, her teeth ready to bite. That's when he realized that he was only a juicy piece of meat to her.

"Babe, please! Don't do this!" Jack cried out.

Linda was not responsive. She was transfixed on his neck alone, and that was the only thing that mattered to her right now. Jack willed himself to shove Linda away from him. She fell backward and hit her head against the bedframe before toppling sideways.

"Shit! Linda, I'm so sorry!" Jack said. "I didn't mean to—"

But Linda had already lunged at him again, falling on her chest trying to grab Jack's feet. Jack stepped back, and Linda crawled toward him. Jack stepped outside the room and closed the door.

A bang came from the other side, followed by clawing and soft gasping. Jack held the doorknob, even though Linda wasn't trying to open the door. She scratched the door with long and soft dragging sounds – Jack assumed it was her nails running across the wooden surface.

"Everything will be okay, baby." Jack said. "Everything will be fine. You'll remember me. You'll remember everything and things will go back to the way they were. I promise."

At the back of his mind, he knew that it was the second promise he would break.

Chapter Twenty

"Come on, Linda. You gotta eat," Jack said.

The canned hamburger sat on the ground in front of Linda. It was as disgusting as Jack imagined it would be. The entire thing was soggy, and the meat was colorless and smelled like feet. Linda hadn't even looked at it.

Jack sat on the chair and sighed deeply. He was becoming desperate. Linda hadn't eaten since yesterday morning, and Jack was starting to get seriously worried. Thoughts raced through his head how his wife would become weaker and weaker, until she perished entirely. He had to do something about it.

But do what, exactly? Going out hunting could be one thing, but wildlife was rarely seen around these parts. All the forest animals seemed to have dispersed under the constant stampeding of the undead hordes. What about bringing an undead for a meal? No, that wouldn't work because for some reason, the undead never ate each other – only the living.

Only the living, reverberated in Jack's mind.

He pushed that thought out of his mind and opened *The Witch of the Woods* to start reading to Linda again. He no longer found the story interesting. Moreover, it was painful for him to read it, but he wanted to continue doing so for Linda's sake. He wanted to help her remember, or to give her a moment of serenity.

She always seemed to calm down when he read the book to her, or when he hummed. She would stare at him the entire time and let out those wheezing breaths, and in those moments, Jack would be sure that he had managed to calm her down, but then he would take a step closer to her and would see her lips twitching and her breathing quickening.

Jack was close to making progress with her, he knew it. Just a little longer, and Linda would move forward from the point of stagnation. That's how it went after she initially died and resurrected.

She was particularly violent and tried attacking him whenever she saw him. Jack had to lure her out of the room and lock her outside while he stayed inside to make the link on the floor that would hold her in place. It was painful for him to treat his wife like she was his prisoner, but he had no other choice.

As time went on, Linda became more and more passive. She refused to eat anything from the pantry, but then Jack brought her favorite rooster, who she named Alfred, upstairs. It was a pure-white rooster that seemed to be the boss of the coop. Whenever it walked, the other chickens dispersed and gave it passage. It looked proud and strong among its peers.

When Jack brought the chicken upstairs to Linda, she stared at it with a sheepish stare. Jack talked to Linda about Alfred, trying to refresh her memory of it. Alfred was always agitated in Jack's presence, but with Linda, he was calm. He would spend an entire hour sitting next to Linda on the couch while she read a book and not once cluck or flap his wings.

Jack put Alfred on the ground and watched as he strode around the room, Linda's gaze fixated on him. Jack decided to leave Alfred in the room with Linda for a little bit. Maybe it would help her. Not a minute after returning downstairs, he heard loud squawking and growling. He ran upstairs to find Linda feeding on Alfred's lifeless body. As frazzled as Jack was, he was also overcome with a sense of clairvoyance. He now knew how to feed Linda, and as costly as it would be for the farm, nothing would be too costly to make his wife happy.

Linda would occasionally try to attack Jack if he got too close, but when he occupied her with a chicken meal, then she would be okay. He figured that she would be aggressive as long as she was hungry because the newly acquired hunger was stronger than her. Jack tried to think of it as a very strong urge to pee. You wanted to do other things, but you couldn't until you relieved yourself.

Then one day, he saw Linda jerking her head toward Jack when he sang for her. He was overcome by happiness, because as meager as it was, it was progress. She was responding to his voice. That urged Jack to spend more time with her and force her to remember more.

He brought all sorts of things into the room that would help her with that – the photo album, the books she read, the clothes she wore for special occasions, the jewelry Jack had bought her, and more.

Jack couldn't be sure, but it looked as if she was responding to some of those items. A tilt of the head, slightly faster or slower breathing, a twitch of an eye – all those things told Jack that there was something going on.

But then the progress stopped. Jack expected Linda to continue improving; maybe to put on a piece of jewelry, or to inspect the dress, or to open the book, or to look at a photo from the album. None of those things happened. One thing he tried the most was cautiously getting closer to her, but whenever he got within bite reach, she would try to sink her teeth into him. Jack realized that he might have been pushing Linda too hard. She still needed time to adjust.

He removed all the items from the room and instead focused on keeping her alive while giving her gentle words of comfort here and there. One day, not long after he had returned from his kidnapping in Eugene, he heard Linda saying something.

It was barely discernible, no more than a gurgle deep in her throat, but Jack thought that it was too much of a coincidence.

J-ck.

Jack jumped of joy. He wanted to run up to Linda and kiss her, but that voracious stare in her eyes told him that he'd best keep his distance still. This was a new level of progress, a new barrier they had broken through.

"Everything's going to be okay, Linda!" he said. "I know it now! You're going to get better! And when you get better, when you no longer feel the need to attack, then we will be able to meet the survivors from the cathedral and they'll see that you're not a danger to anyone!"

On his way out, Jack grabbed the chair to move it out of the way and he felt sharp pain in his finger. He winced and jerked his hand back as if burned by the stove and saw blood coming out of his forefinger. He pricked himself on the small tip of the nail that jutted out of the chair.

Behind him, he heard Linda screaming and the chain clinking as she strained against it. Jack turned his head to see Linda's arms outstretched toward Jack. She was baring her teeth, her eyes wide with fury and madness. Jack looked down at his bleeding forefinger.

He stretched his arm to the side as far as he could. Linda's eyes remained fixated on the finger, and not on him. Jack let his arm fall limply against his side, lost for words, and overcome by immense sadness. He turned around and strode out of the room, locking it behind him. Even with the door closed, Linda continued snarling.

Jack went downstairs and turned on the radio. Music from Gary's channel played, and it helped Jack relax. As he stared out the window, the clouds congealed in the sky and rain started.

For the first time ever, Jack felt alone on the farm. He had grown so accustomed to the chickens being in the coop that the absence of the occasional clucking coming from the back of the house felt imposing. Linda was upstairs, but it felt as if she wasn't. Jack tried to imagine what they would have been doing now if she hadn't been infected.

On a rainy day like this one, they would probably snuggle up together in bed and listen to the rain until they fell asleep. Jack felt a wave of sadness incoming, and he fought hard to suppress it. What he wouldn't give to have that moment of tranquility with Linda – to have her lying on his chest and sleeping while he listened to her steady breathing.

Jack fell asleep much faster than he thought he would.

****

He knew that he was dreaming because he saw himself in his dream in an out-of-body experience, as if watching someone else on TV. In the dream, Jack opened the door to Linda's room and stepped inside. He stared at Linda, and Linda stared back at him. The Jack observing the situation knew that the Jack in the room was about to do something bad, even though he couldn't tell what.

Without thinking, Jack took a fervent step toward Linda and hugged her. Linda bit him in the neck. Blood gushed out, but Jack didn't flinch. He continued embracing Linda in a bear hug while she took a bite after bite. Blood abundantly spurted out of Jack's missing chunk of neck and pooled on the floor around their feet.

The entire floor was covered in a layer of blood, and the level grew, engulfing Jack and Linda from the feet up until the entire room was submerged and all the observer could see was shades of dark red.

Jack woke up with a start. It was dark. Rain drummed on the roof of the house, and soft classical music played on the radio. Jack felt as if he had just woken up from a century-long coma. He walked over to the window and looked outside. He could hardly see anything, but he thought he detected meager movement in the meadow – a straggler here and there. No one was at the fence, though.

A rumble in his stomach told him that it was time for him to eat. He had only eaten one can of tuna earlier today, and he felt like he could eat an entire turkey. On nights like these when he or Linda had hankerings, they would drive to a diner close to Eugene for chicken wings or pancakes. That was something that always happened late at night, usually after ten PM, but there have been a couple of times when he heard Linda rummaging through the fridge downstairs at one AM like a raccoon.

Whenever he woke up to see that, he asked her what she felt like eating. Whether she knew or didn't know, the answer was always in the diner. In fact, they had gone to that place only at night, and Jack often joked that the diner only existed after sundown, and that it disappeared in the morning.

Jack wondered for a moment if the diner was still there, or if it had been overrun by the undead – or worse. He hoped that it was still okay. The place didn't harbor any special sanctuary that it could provide to the survivors, nor did it hold any supplies of significance, but it had a special place in Jack's heart.

He sat at the kitchen table and opened a can of vegetables in tomato sauce. Jack didn't like having a meatless dinner, but he didn't care about what he ate tonight – he just needed something to stop the painful rumbling in his belly. He felt a little bad for eating while Linda was upstairs without food, but going on a hunger strike would do neither of them any good.

He thought about what to do in order to keep Linda fed, but no inspiration came to him. He could go to the town and kill some of those raiders, but it was too risky. Last time, he got lucky. The next time, he might run into a bigger group. Plus, he couldn't keep lugging dead bodies back to the farm so that Linda could eat.

And she ate those two so damn fast!

The music on the radio stopped and Gary's pleasant voice took over.

"The weather's not very good out there tonight, folks. Try to stay inside because you might catch hypothermia in the rain. That is unless the walking dead don't get to you first. But if you're feeling especially brave, you can use the cover of the rain to sneak past the hordes unseen and check out those swarmed buildings in your neighborhood that you're sure have some hidden caches of food, meds, and ammo. Or you can get the drop on your neighbor and raid their house. But who would want to do that? They'd be a dick."

Jack snorted in laughter.

"We're getting reports that people are still trying to reach the military checkpoint in Veneta every day, and every day, they're dying. If you're out there listening to this, please, hear us out. Do not go to the Veneta checkpoint. The military is no longer there, and even while they were, they were killing civilians indiscriminately. They shot men, women, and children for so much as having a small scratch!" Gary raised his tone, and Jack detected anger in it. "They killed the people who trusted them, and then they abandoned the checkpoint. But karma always comes back to bite you in the ass, because that same group of soldiers got ambushed by a humongous horde at *Swanson Brothers Lumber* and wiped out to the last man. Justice has been served, people."

Silence filled the air for a moment. Jack had finished scraping the remainder of the food and sauce from the bottom of the can and was now sitting and listening to the radio show attentively.

"Our latest reports say that a huge horde of undead lumberjacks and soldiers is now headed East, back toward Veneta, and will most likely end up in Eugene and Springfield. Anyone in Eugene listening to this, don't panic just yet. The horde won't be there for at least another two days. Pack your things, move out of the way and wait for the horde to pass. By then, we'll have more information for you, folks, about our safe haven. Don't lose hope. Gary out."

The music continued, leaving Jack in a deeply contemplative state. He tapped his fingers on the table while looking into empty space. Gary's words reverberated in his skull like a catchy tune. *People are trying to reach Veneta every day, and every day, they're dying.*

Jack hated himself for considering the plan that had been swirling in his mind. As if to further convince him, scratching came from upstairs. That was the answer enough for Jack. Eugene was more dangerous than the road to Veneta. If things got really bad there, he could just turn his car around and bolt out of there. The scratching became louder.

Just hold on until tomorrow, Linda. I'll get you some food, Jack thought to himself with slight uncertainty.

Chapter Twenty-One

He was never a man who could spend too much time with other people. An hour with someone, and he would already start to feel drained. And yet, with her, no amount of time they spent together was enough. He could have his alone time even when she was with him in the room. That's how he knew that she was the one.

"So, I heard you work in an antique shop, Jack," Linda's dad said and put a piece of steak on his fork into his mouth.

Jack detected spite in his voice. It was the kind of tone he heard from rich people who came into the shop and treated Jack like he was less human just because he worked a job that many people considered a dead-end.

"That's right, Grant," Jack replied. Linda's dad slightly furrowed his nose at the mention of his name. He looked at his wife Martha who sat next to him, and then back at Jack. He maintained the stare for a moment while chewing, before gravitating his gaze to the plate with the food.

Jack looked at Linda's mom, who had been staring at him this entire time, as well. As soon as their eyes met, she looked down. Jack felt immensely uncomfortable in their presence. He felt as if he were being scrutinized under a microscope.

Linda had talked to Jack about her parents many times before, and he hadn't heard too many good things. They were very strict toward Linda when she was younger. Martha was a doctor in Springfield, and Grant worked as a structural engineer, so naturally, expectations for their only daughter were high.

When Linda told them that she hadn't planned on finishing anything past a bachelor's degree, they were, of course, disappointed. They used every opportunity they could at family gatherings to point to other relatives and say things like, "Look, there's your cousin Emily, she just graduated from Harvard", or "Have you said hi to Joshua? He started his own business a few years ago."

Linda ignored them for the most part, but they invaded her life with good-intended advice whenever they had the opportunity. Their relationship further strained when Linda started dating Jack. For an engineer and a doctor who had six-figure salaries, having their daughter date a guy with a minimum-wage job was a low blow. They often said so openly to Linda, and then Linda mentioned it in passing to Jack.

Don't worry about them, Jack. I don't care what they think about you.

But Jack cared, because he knew that his and Linda's life would only be difficult if the parents didn't accept Jack as part of the family. He was also afraid that the parents might influence Linda into leaving Jack. Linda was smart, much smarter than Jack, he thought, and he was afraid that one day she would realize that she could do better.

In fact, Linda had wooers every day. People who came to her work hit on her daily, and that made Jack immensely jealous, but when he saw how uninterested she was in each and every one of them – even the rich successful handsome guys in suits – he stopped worrying. He also saw the way she looked at him, and that made him realize that Linda didn't care about the money, or academic success, or anything like that.

She loved Jack for being Jack.

"You're actively looking for a new job, right?" Grant asked. "Working in an antique shop is great for pocket money, but we all have to grow up some day. You agree with me, right?" He smiled when he said that, but Jack couldn't have felt more humiliated.

"Dad," Linda said sternly from her seat next to Jack. "I think what Jack does, is his own concern. There's nothing wrong with working in a shop."

Jack couldn't help but feel extremely cared for and loved when Linda jumped to his defense like that.

"No, that's fine," Martha said. "But you kids need some financial support. You can't rely on the parents to give you money." She grinned and looked at Jack. "I assume you have to borrow money from your parents, correct, Jack?"

"I don't have a good relationship with my parents, actually." He regretted saying that as soon as the words left his mouth, but it was already too late.

"Oh, I see. And why is that?" Martha asked. Jack suddenly felt like he was being questioned by a psychologist.

"Mom!" Linda raised her tone.

"I'm just curious, sweetie. No need to get upset." The mom smiled.

Jack didn't like talking about his parents, so he had no idea why he blurted out that he had a bad relationship with them.

"Never mind about the parents, Martha," Grant said. "I'm more interested in the prospect of the future. Tell me, Jack. What are your plans?"

Jack wasn't sure if the question referred to his plans with Linda, or his plans in general.

"Well, I am building my own farm outside Eugene. So, I was hoping to one day be able to move in over there." He wanted to add that he would be moving in with Linda, but he wasn't sure what the reaction of the parents would be, so he refrained from doing so.

Grant took another bite of his steak and averted his gaze from Jack. His facial expression looked like he was trying to chew a piece of tire. The mother also looked down.

"The farm is actually almost finished. It just needs a good gate, and some windows, and then the furniture, but um… yeah." Jack's voice trailed off when he failed to get a reaction from the parents.

"So, you plan on paying for the farm with the money you earn from your job?" Grant asked with a hint of irony in his timbre.

"Jack is a hard-working man, Dad," Linda said. "Aside from the antique shop, he also works part-time as a mechanic, and on the weekends, he and I volunteer on the Johnson farmstead, so we can learn more before we move in together." She gently put a hand on Jack's thigh under the table. Jack squeezed his hand over hers.

"I'm sorry," Grant said as he loudly dropped his fork and knife into the plate. "I just don't see how you two plan to survive like this. I mean, maybe I'm wrong. But living on the farm? We're way past that. It's the twenty-first century, for crying out loud."

"So, farms are no longer needed?" Linda asked ironically.

"If you plan to have children someday, then you would want to raise them in an environment where they can grow up to be normal, surrounded by other children, in a city that has access to everything."

"Thank you for the warning, Dad, but I think Jack and I are old enough to know what we should and shouldn't do." Linda flashed her dad a rictus.

The rest of the dinner continued in awkward silence. When it was finally over, they spent some time sitting in the living room with the TV on. Jack remained quiet the entire time. At one point, Martha went into the kitchen and called Linda to come help her. Jack was uncomfortable staying alone in the room with Grant, but luckily, after a minute of deafening silence, Grant stood up and went to see what was going on in the kitchen.

A few minutes had gone by, and that's when Jack heard voices coming from the kitchen. The voices were indiscernible, but among them, he could distinctly hear Grant's bellowing.

"He's not right for you!" he shouted among other things.

Jack tip-toed to the kitchen door and eavesdropped on the conversation. He only heard parts of sentences coming from all three family members.

"You need to go back to school and–"

"Why don't you try finding someone from–"

"I'm not going to–"

"What about Vincent? He's a nice guy, and he works as–"

"Mom, will you stop and list–"

"A farm, for Christ's sake!"

And then Linda's voice cut through the other two like knife through butter, silencing the room. "That's enough! I love Jack, and I am not going to break up with him because you want me to. I don't care about his job. I don't care that you think he's a stupid farmer. I love him and I'm going to spend the rest of my life with him."

"Linda, your mother and I only want what's best for you," Grant said with a tone of finality. "But if you continue to go against our wishes, then we will be very, very disappointed." That sentence sounded more like a threat.

Silence fell on the room for a moment before Linda spoke up again. "Like I already said – I love him more than I've ever loved anyone or anything. So, you either learn to accept him as your own, or we can stop communicating altogether."

Jack felt a warm sensation in his chest. It wasn't until then that he truly realized how much Linda loved him. She was putting Jack before her own parents. That was true love. More voices ensued, this time hushed, but Jack tip-toed back to the living room.

Linda walked out of the kitchen a moment later, her cheeks ruddy, and an intense look on her face. "Everything okay, babe?" Jack asked.

"Yeah," she said. "Listen, um… we should go. I think I forgot to lock my apartment, and I wanna go back to check it."

"Yeah, sure," Jack said as he stood up.

The parents walked into the living room a moment later, dismal looks on their faces. Grant tried to hide it by smiling and telling Linda to visit whenever she wanted. He didn't even look at Jack. On the drive back home, Jack tried to pretend he hadn't heard the conversation in the kitchen, but the more he tried to act natural, the more rigid his behavior was.

"So, why the abrupt leave?" Jack asked, trying not to give away that he already knew.

"I'm just feeling tired," Linda said. "And I want to have some us time." She put a hand on his thigh and smiled. Jack looked at her. He fell in love with her all over again.

"What?" she asked, oblivious.

Jack stopped the truck at the first red traffic light and used the opportunity to lean toward Linda and kiss her.

"I love you," he said.

Chapter Twenty-Two

Jack made sure to inspect the weapons he had. There was a handgun that the young guy who broke into his home had, and a gun that the woman was using. They had some ammunition in the car, but it wasn't much. Jack also had the assault rifle, but it only had fifteen bullets left. He opted for the Glock since it had the most bullets.

He didn't pack much – a bottle of water, and a hatchet. The car that the gang members had used to get to his farm still had a lot of gas in it, and since it was generally a better vehicle than his truck, he opted to use the truck as much as he could before switching to the new car. The car was smaller than his pickup, which meant easier navigation on the road, but Jack assumed that it wouldn't really make a huge difference on the highway since it would most likely be packed with abandoned vehicles.

The morning was sunny, and the rain from last night had stopped entirely. It was cold, but less than what Jack expected. There were two undead at the fence that he needed to clear out, but he didn't bother driving them to the woods to put them on a pile.

When he drove the truck out and closed the fence behind him, he stopped and thought about the best route to take to reach the highway. He opted for the dirt road that led West of Eugene and directly onto the Florence Eugene Highway, since he figured it would be the least crowded place.

Jack thought about saying goodbye to Linda and letting her walk the house, but he didn't want another incident like the last time. He hoped that it wouldn't come to it again that someone would break into the house, and if they did, that Linda would remain safely locked in her room.

With that thought, he stepped on the gas pedal, and the truck lurched forward. The vehicle produced unsettling scraping sounds from somewhere, and Jack knew that it probably meant that something was wrong with the engine. He hoped that the truck would last until returning home.

Even on the unpaved road leading to the highway, there were abandoned cars and a couple of undead. The highway was an entirely different story. He was able to drive the truck for a short time, but then the road became backed up with so many cars that there was no way Jack would be able to even squeeze between with the truck, let alone turn around and change directions. It was clear that the drivers had been in a panic to cause such a state of chaos.

Cars strayed out of their lanes, crashing into other vehicles, at some points completely cutting off access to the rest of the road. Dead bodies littered the vehicles and concrete alike, making the place look more like a mass grave than a highway. Jack stopped the truck and killed the engine.

He would need to walk from here, and he was sure that others who tried reaching the checkpoint had walked, too. The question was, how far did they make it before getting stopped by the undead? It would take at least a few hours of walking to reach the Veneta checkpoint.

Jack didn't need to go that far. He just needed one fresh body to cut up so that he could bring it to Linda. If he had to walk for hours every day to feed her, then this plan wouldn't work.

Feeling a sense of dread already creeping up on him, Jack turned on the engine, made a U-turn, and then turned it off again. He pulled out the keys, took his bottle of water, hatchet, and pistol, and stepped outside.

It was much chillier here for some reason. Strong gusts of wind blew in his face before stopping entirely for protracted moments. Jack took a sip of water and put it in the pocket of his jacket. The pistol was in his jeans, and the hatchet in his hand. He wouldn't use his gun here unless he really had to, because it might draw the undead to him.

The first thing he did was climb on one of the vans to survey the highway. In the distance, he could see a few undead roaming. He counted three. He jumped off and gripped the hatchet more tightly.

Just one body. That's all he needed to find.

Jack sniffled and took a confident step forward. The lyrics from a famous rock song singing about a highway comically entered his mind, and he suppressed them to focus on the mission. The cars were so close to each other that Jack had to sidle between them at some points, and jump over them in the other. He saw at least five undead trapped in the cars while passing – when they saw Jack, they pressed against the window, smearing blood all over it in an attempt to get to him. Jack ignored them.

Outside the road, firs and pines stretched upward like needles, at some points revealing vast landscapes of golden grass, at others completely obscuring the view with their foliage. Jack detected the undead slinking between the trees, just barely discernible silhouettes that nagged his peripheral vision enough for him to jerk his head toward them.

Among the ruins of the highway, he also ran into the undead who roamed the road. Rather than risk his life by walking away from them, he took care of them by hitting them in the head with the hatchet. After each kill, he wiped the blade on the clothes of the corpses.

He kept a fervent eye out for fresh dead bodies, but everything he had seen up until that point was half-rotted or still walking. Even after one whole hour of the grueling trek on the highway, he hadn't seen a single body that he could bring back to Linda for a meal.

By then, he was exhausted from the climbing, hopping, and squeezing. His focus was also off, and he knew that he couldn't afford dropping his guard, especially since he was about to enter a tunnel. On top of everything, he was cold. The wind had been whipping him from all sides, and his hands had gone slightly numb from the cold.

Jack decided to take a break for a little bit. He inspected the nearby cars and found one that had no corpses or visible blood stains inside. He also made sure to check the backseat of the car for any lurking dead bodies.

As soon as he sat inside and closed the door, he started to feel a little better. The squall of wind that whistled outside was now muffled, but Jack could still clearly hear it. It intermittently went quieter and louder, circling him like a shark, tantalizing him.

Jack looked in the rearview mirror. It was so dirty that he couldn't see anything in it. He decided not to touch it. Ahead of him were a few more undead. Jack ran a hand through his hair, feeling exasperated. He had a long way to go, and he would have an even longer way to go back the way he came.

But then he remembered Linda. She was at home, in her room, just standing there. Jack wondered what she felt like right now. Was she hungry? Lonely? Scared? Did she feel anything at all?

Whenever he thought of her, he couldn't help but get an accompanying pang of something painful in his heart. That pang hadn't been here up until a couple of days ago, and Jack's mind reeled to understand what was causing such dread to rise in him whenever he thought about his wife.

You're scared. You're scared because you know she's not making any progress. You think she's going to stay like this forever, only getting worse with each passing day until she ceases to exist entirely.

The voice was like a reality check for Jack, but he refused to listen to it.

No, she's getting better, another voice in his head intervened. *Just a few days ago, she said my name. She remembers who I am.*

No, she doesn't. That was just a sound in her throat. Linda can't speak anymore. And remember how she lunged at you when you cut your finger?

Jack found no way to refute that, as much as he wanted to. Lately, his deeply buried doubts started surfacing, and he buried them back inside, but they kept poking out, like persistent roots that grew out of the ground over and over.

As much as Jack didn't want to admit it, he started to wonder if the life that Linda lived right now was the right way to live. Whenever he looked at her, that thought gnawed at him from somewhere in the deepest recesses of his being, not enough for him to know what it is, but just enough to remind him that something was there.

He went from firmly believing that Linda was still there, to wondering if ending Linda's life would be the merciful thing to do. That was only a faraway thought, though. Jack would never put Linda down like an animal. He would never be able to live with himself.

I'm just tired, that's all. I'm tired and cold, and that makes people depressed. As soon as I get some shuteye, those bad thoughts will disappear.

Suddenly, being out there in the cold wind felt more welcoming than being trapped inside the car with his own thoughts. Jack opened the door and stepped out. He suddenly felt emotionally drained, but he couldn't stop. He had to keep going.

The sun hid behind the clouds once again, giving the sky a tinge of gray. He hoped it wouldn't start raining. Jack entered the tunnel, and suddenly felt like a moron for not bringing a flashlight. Momentarily, he was blinded when he stepped into the shadows of the cold concrete surrounding him, but slowly his eyes adjusted.

In here was an even greater mess. A school bus had toppled sideways and was blocking much of the road. Jack had to walk on the side of the tunnel, doing his best to ignore the scratching sounds coming from inside the bus. He heard groaning coming from the tunnel, echoing and bouncing off the walls. It was difficult to tell where the sound was coming from in such enclosed space. It could have been from two hundred feet away, or from two feet away.

Jack gripped the hatchet more firmly and made his way through the tunnel. He ran into one undead pinned with a car against the wall. Its legs were crushed beyond recognition, but the tendons still held on firmly, holding the person rooted to the place. Its groans grew louder when it saw Jack, and in the tunnel, the voice seemed to be carried in every direction, reaching a crescendo that never came. Jack killed it with the hatchet – half of the reason was because its groans unnerved him, the other half was to avoid attracting others.

The tunnel wasn't long, and soon, Jack was out of it, once again facing the bleak sky above his head. He never felt so relieved to see such bad weather. He walked for another thirty minutes or so while disposing of the undead. He had killed another eight, if he counted correctly, when he was forced to stop.

He heard them before he saw them.

In the distance, a congregation of the undead, what looked like hundreds of them, clustered the road. They bumped into each other, tripped, and crawled, all the while producing a bevy of noises that filled the air even at such a distance.

Jack would not be able to go any further. That brought him a sense of alleviation, but also worry. He would need to go back home empty-handed. No, that would not work. He would find something for Linda to eat, even if it was a meager meal.

He looked around him and saw the dead body of an old man propped with its back against the railing on the side of the road. Jack hadn't seen him before. The old man had a trickle of dried blood from the top of his head crusted down his grizzled hair and behind his ear. His skin color still looked healthy, unlike the pallid ones that the undead had. He looked like he might have died just recently.

Okay, that will have to do, Jack thought.

He cautiously approached the old man while gripping his axe tightly. The thought of hacking through this dead person's limbs made Jack feel queasy. The job would get nasty, there was no doubt about it, but he had to do it. He could hack off both arms and both legs, and Linda might have a day's worth of a meal.

As soon as Jack knelt beside the body, his mind conjured up images of the hatchet blade digging through the poor old man's leg with squelching sounds, and blood spurting everywhere like a fountain. No, he was dead, so at least the blood wouldn't be running everywhere, Jack hoped.

He placed a hand on the man's knee and gently put the blade on the man's thigh, trying to figure out what would be the best place to cut. He naturally wanted to get as much meat as possible, so as close to the crotch as possible.

Jack raised the hatchet above his head and inhaled sharply. Before he could bring the blade down, something happened that interrupted his butchering action. The old man let out a soft moan and raised one hand toward Jack. Jack screamed and recoiled backward, falling on his rear in the process.

He scooted out of reach of the dead body, and then shot up to his feet with readiness. The old man looked at Jack, and his arm limply fell back on the floor.

"Goddammit," Jack said with a scoff.

Another undead. He shook his head and looked left at the group of undead. Was it just him, or were they getting closer? Not only that, but was there more of them than Jack initially thought? Ignoring the old man's hungry gaze, Jack climbed the hood of the closest car and squinted toward the group of undead.

"Oh, Christ," Jack said.

It wasn't hundreds of them. What Jack saw earlier was merely a small part of the group at the front.

All the way as far as Jack could see, the undead littered the highway, like people at a rock concert. And they were moving toward him. Although they were slow, Jack didn't have a lot of time left. He had to get back to his car and return to the farm.

He jumped off the hood of the car. Just as he took a step in the direction which he came from, his action was interrupted once more.

"Help me," a gruff voice said.

Chapter Twenty-Three

All the things related to the future that seemed so big and scary were no longer daunting. Quite the opposite. The more he spent time with her, the more he couldn't wait for them to start their future and to plan things together.

"Alright, I got you your mushrooms and berries," Jack said to Linda.

He found her at the back of the house, doing something with a plant in a flowerpot. She had a sunhat on and wore yellow latex gloves. The chickens were outside the coop, walking around her at a safe distance – except Alfred. He curiously peeked toward the plant pot a few times before stalking off.

"You didn't eat any of them, did you?" Linda asked.

"Just a nibble here and there," Jack said as he placed the full basket on the ground in front of her.

Linda gently rummaged through the basket, showing excitement at each new berry or mushroom she discovered in the basket.

"So, anything deadly in there?" Jack asked.

"I'm not going to let you know if I plan on poisoning you, Jack. It would ruin the assassination attempt."

"No, it wouldn't. If you put the poison in your stew, I would eat it even if you told me that it's poisoned."

Linda laughed. Jack squatted down to take a better look at the flowerpot. He saw something tiny and green sprouting out from the dirt.

"Wow," he said. "You really know how to grow plants."

"Yeah. Unbelievable that they taught us that in the botanist school, huh?" Linda joked.

Now it was Jack's turn to laugh. Seeing Linda nurturing the plants so carefully and helping them grow made him see her in a different light.

"You would make a wonderful mother," Jack blurted.

"What?" Linda looked from the basket at Jack.

Jack gulped, just then realizing the stupidity of his words. He didn't want Linda to get the wrong idea.

"Um, I mean… You know, with the way you nurture plants and all that, it's really nice. You looked like you have a motherly instinct." He understood that that sentence sounded even more stupid, but it was too late to take it back.

Linda flashed Jack a fascinated smile. "Are you saying you would like to have children with me, kind sir?" she asked.

Jack felt a pang of relief. He chuckled and said, "Well, I mean, if I could choose someone to mother my children, then yes, I would choose you. You seem like a cool person and all."

Linda pressed her lips tightly. She looked like she was trying not to burst into a laughing fit.

"Does that make you uncomfortable, Lin?" Jack asked.

Linda shook her head. "Whenever your mom showed me the photo album of you as a kid, I get this really strong feeling of wanting a mini-Jack running around the farm."

"I'd prefer a mini-Linda, to tell you the truth."

Linda turned to face the flowerpot. She picked it up and stood up. "Let's see if we can't get this little fella to grow first." She turned to Jack. "And then, maybe we can work on a mini-Jack or mini-Linda."

She offered no other elaboration before turning around to leave. Jack stood up and put his hands on his hips. He could suddenly envision a little girl running alongside Linda, asking her curiously about the plant, while Linda explained in simplified terminology what it meant and showing her how to take care of the plant. Jack also imagined feeding the chickens and a little boy standing by his side, excitedly tossing the corn to the fowl for the first time in his life.

Jack couldn't wipe the smile off his face.

Chapter Twenty-Four

At first, Jack thought it was just his imagination. He looked toward the old man slumped against the railing and saw him still transfixed on Jack, but his mouth was closed. He couldn't have possibly uttered that sentence, right?

They were locked in a staring contest, and then the old man raised his hand again. "Please, don't leave me here," he said with a raspy voice.

Jack thought he was dreaming. He felt like he was in one of those movies that he watched as a child where the protagonist discovers something astounding – like that their pets can talk, or that there is a portal inside their closet.

The old man turned his head to the source of the oncoming horde, and then back to Jack. "Just help me stand, please," the old man said.

"You… you're not dead?" Jack asked.

"I'm talking, aren't I?"

Jack couldn't help but think that this was a trick of some sort. Maybe an advanced undead that still had his cognitive functioning skills. For a long moment, all he could do was stare at the old man. The man looked in the direction of the horde again, and then back at Jack.

"They're getting closer, come on! Please!" he shouted.

Even with the raised tone, Jack could now hardly hear him from the horde that was now much closer. It was the thousands of morphed voices of the undead wave ready to sweep anything in their path that pushed Jack into action.

Jack ran up to the old man and grabbed him by the hand. He pulled him up with a lot of effort – he was slightly heavier. The old man groaned, and Jack hoped that he wasn't causing more damage to him with the yank. Jack pulled him up so hard that the old man took an unsteady step forward and slightly bent over. Jack got ready to grab him in case the man's legs buckled under him.

"Thank you." The old man looked at him wearily.

The first lines of the undead were less than a hundred feet away. They had spotted Jack and the old man and were already outstretching their arms forward, trying to reach the prey in front of them.

"We need to go," Jack said. "Can you walk?"

The old man nodded. Jack took the lead and began fast-walking down the way he came. He looked back at the old man to see if he was following. He was slower, and his walk looked awkward with the way he swung his arms back and forth. He reminded Jack of the old people he saw fast-walking on marathon races, except this guy looked more like he was just learning how to walk.

"I'm right behind you, just keep going!" the old man said with a bouncy voice from the gait.

Slowly, they were putting the distance between themselves and the horde. They were still in danger though, and Jack knew that they couldn't stop for more than a few seconds, otherwise the undead might catch up to them.

It took everything in Jack not to break into a sprint and leave the old man behind, but he couldn't do it. He couldn't even be sure if the man was a good person or not, but he was vulnerable, and Jack's instinct told him that he should help him.

No, it wasn't Jack's instinct. It was Linda's instinct transferred onto Jack. She always helped the ones who needed it, much more than Jack. Whether it was a hungry stray animal, or donations for charity, or even helping an old person carry their groceries, Linda was always there to help.

Jack had never met a person who got so happy when doing something for other people. When she bought presents for other people, she got excited as if the present was for her. She'd often return home and tell Jack she did something bad. He always asked, "Who did you help this time?" and then she proceeded to tell him what she did for a person in need and how much it cost. She asked Jack if he was mad at her for doing so, but Jack never got mad at her for that. He saw how happy it made her, and that made him happy, too. It also made him fall in love with her more.

But then he hated her for it. Her kindness was her undoing in the end. She tried helping bad people, and she died because of it. Jack looked back at the old man again. He couldn't tell from his face if he was a good man or not. Maybe Jack should just leave him here and go back to the farm. It was every man for himself, anyway.

The old man looked back at the horde, and then increased his pace just a little bit. He already looked like he was dying from exhaustion.

"Come on, hurry up," Jack urged him as he jumped over a car blocking the path.

The old man clumsily and slowly climbed, but he was able to cross to the other side. Now that they were past the blockade, they should have a little more time until the horde caught up. The undead would climb over each other on the car, and many would end up crushed under the weight of their fellow horde members, but the horde would continue going.

The highway would be inaccessible after today. The horde would leave a lot of stragglers behind, and it would probably be too dangerous to return here. It didn't matter anyway, because there was nothing on this stretch of the road. Just like Gary said – Veneta has been overrun.

"You okay?" Jack asked as he turned toward the old guy.

"Yes. I just need to… just need to slow down… for a moment," the man said, winded.

"We can slow down, but we can't stop. They're still too close."

"I know."

Jack looked back at the army of zombies. Their moans were distant now, and their attention seemed to drop from Jack and the old man. They walked forward, but their arms weren't outstretched in front of them anymore.

"Thank you for saving me back there," the old man said. "Very convenient that you arrived when you did. A minute later I would have been picked to the bone."

"Yeah. I'm Jack, by the way."

"I'm William."

"What happened to you, William?"

"I was trying to reach the checkpoint, just like everyone on this highway. But then the group I traveled with decided that I was only slowing them down and decided to knock me out, take my things, and leave me behind."

"Hm."

"The ungrateful bastards. They didn't complain when their kid needed medical help. But then they no longer needed me, so they got rid of me."

"Medical help? Are you a doctor?"

"I used to be, yes. But I'm retired now."

Jack felt his heart leaping against his chest. A doctor. He could help Linda. Jack couldn't help but get his hopes up, even though the rational part of him told him to keep them in check. He felt like he could sprint all the way back to the car and not get tired.

"Well, the checkpoint has been overrun. That's what the guy on the radio said days ago. So, the group you traveled with is most likely dead if they walked straight into that." Jack hooked a thumb over his shoulder toward the horde.

"Really?" William's face turned grievous. "We have functioning radio stations? I didn't know that."

"Yeah. They're apparently organizing some kind of a safe place for survivors."

"Where?"

"No idea. They had one in the cathedral of Eugene, but then the raiders took it."

"Such a shame."

Thirty minutes later, the horde was much more distant, their moans heard only when Jack perked up his ears. He and William sat to take a short break after making it through the tunnel. By then, Jack's feet were killing him and the moment of rest was more than welcome. The doctor held on pretty well, despite looking like he would break into pieces at the slightest fall.

"I'm sorry, can I trouble you for some of that water?" William asked.

Jack handed him the bottle. The doctor drank almost half of it before returning the bottle to Jack and thanking him.

"Do you have a safe place to stay?" he asked.

"Yeah. I live on a farm close to Eugene. You're welcome to stay there. It's as safe as it gets," Jack said.

"Thank you." William nodded briskly. "I only need a few days to recover, and then I'll be on my way. Do you live with someone there?"

Jack opened his mouth, but then closed it. He looked back at the horde, whose voices had grown closer. He then turned back to the doctor.

"No. I live alone," Jack said after a moment of hesitation.

William nodded slowly, but kept his eyes fixated on Jack. Jack stood up with alacrity. "We should go," he said. "The horde's getting closer."

Both Jack and William were glad to finally reach the pickup. By then, the horde was nowhere in sight, and could not be heard, either. Jack turned the key in the ignition. The truck produced sounds of contact, but didn't turn on. *Shit.* Jack tried again, and on the third try, the engine whirred to life. Jack stepped on the gas and they drove off. William huffed, and then leaned back in the passenger seat and closed his eyes for a moment.

"My God, what an ordeal," he exclaimed theatrically before turning to Jack. "What were you doing out there, anyway?"

"Looking for supplies," Jack lied.

"I see," William nodded.

"We'll be at the farm soon. The guy on the radio said that the horde's gonna go through Eugene, but it'll be a while until they reach it. There are also a lot of survivors in Eugene, so the horde might linger there."

"Any news from the government?"

"None."

They spent the rest of the ride in silence. Jack felt oddly optimistic about everything, and he knew that he was simply grasping onto the smallest straws he could find in order to retain hope.

He had no food for Linda, but he had something better that might help cure her permanently.

Chapter Twenty-Five

She was one of a kind. She was uncorrupted despite life trying so hard to corrupt her. She saw good in everything and everyone, and that, in turn, caused everyone around her to become a better person. Especially him.

"Happy Birthday, Jack!" Linda shouted.

She presented him with a box wrapped in red decorative paper. Jack looked down at the box, and then up at Linda.

"I thought we said no presents, Linda," he said with a smirk on his face.

"I know. But it's your birthday. I can't just not buy you anything." Linda rolled her eyes.

"But I only asked for–"

"I know," Linda said and took a step closer to him. She tugged him closer by the shirt until their lips were inches apart, and whispered, "You'll get that present after dinner, Mr. Impatient."

Jack smiled and kissed her. He took the box from her and went to sit on the couch. Linda sat next to him and stared at him with an impatient glare. She wanted him to open the present right here, right now. Jack held the box in both hands, gently, because he had no idea how fragile the item inside was.

It was a small box, so he assumed that the item was something expensive. He already prepared a speech to give to Linda about not spending so much money on him. He carefully unwrapped the box and removed the decorative paper, doing his best not to rip it. The paper on the box was just as important to Jack as the gift inside, because both came from Linda.

"Oh, wow," Jack said when he beheld the white box under the wrapping paper. He looked at Linda, whose smile was so wide that if it were wider, it would go all around her head.

"Go on, open it," Linda said.

Jack removed the lid on the box and stared at the fancy wristwatch inside. It was black and emblazoned with so many dials inside the casing that Jack had trouble understanding which one showed the time.

"Wow," he said again.

"Put it on," Linda tapped him on the shoulder.

Jack removed the watch from the box and closed it around his wrist. He hated to say it, but it looked awesome.

"It looks so great on you," Linda said.

"You say that about everything I put on. I could wear a bracelet made of animal bones and you'd like it."

"Ew," Linda winkled her nose.

Jack leaned in and kissed her. "Thanks, babe," he said.

"You like it?" Linda asked.

"Of course."

"You always say that. I could buy you a watch made from animal bones and you'd like it," Linda retorted.

"I like everything you get me, even if it's a piece of rock," Jack said and kissed her again.

"Good to know. Next year I'll save the money and just get you a rock, instead."

Jack leaned to the side of the couch and reached for something on the floor.

"Well, I knew you were going to buy me the watch because you saw me saying that it looks cool when we walked past the store the other day, so…" Jack said as he straightened his back and presented a big open box to Linda.

Linda looked at the box with a frown, her lips contorting into a smile. "Honey? What is that?" she asked skeptically.

"Peek inside and see," Jack said.

"You bought me a present for your birthday?" Linda looked at him and took the box.

Jack shrugged. He put the box on Linda's lap. She moved the flaps on the top aside and looked into the box. A high-pitched chirp came from inside, and Linda immediately widened her eyes and gasped.

"Oh. My. God," she said as she dug both hands into the box.

A moment later, she brought them out, and in the palms of her hand was a baby chick. The animal was small and round, its head barely discernible from the body, and it remained perfectly still in Linda's hand.

"Look at its color. It's completely white!" Linda said, and then turned to the chick. "Hey there, little guy. You're a cute little guy, aren't you?" She brought the chick up to her cheek and smiled. "Geez, it's so fluffy."

Seeing Linda so affectionate with the baby chick made Jack all warm inside. The wristwatch was a nice present, but seeing Linda happy was better.

"Where did you get him?" she asked.

"From the Johnson farmstead," Jack said. "They had a bunch and gave me a bunch."

"Wait, a bunch?" Linda asked.

Jack stood up and gestured with his head toward the door. He led Linda to the previously empty chicken coop. The coop boomed with tiny chirping noises, and when they approached, Linda gasped again. A lamp was pointed at the coop and in it were dozens of baby chicks, running all around the place like yellow furry balls.

All were yellow, with some having a slightly faded color, but only the one from the box was white. Jack specifically chose that one to show to Linda first because it was unique. When Linda saw the coop, she darted her eyes around the interior of it, looking like she didn't know what to do with herself.

"Jack!" she looked at her husband. "Do you realize what this means?"

"No. What?"

"We have our own animals! These are our first animals on *our* farm!" Linda exclaimed with a petulant and jovial voice.

Jack put an arm around her shoulder. "Well, these are only the *first* animals. We'll get more in the future. Maybe some goats, and guard dogs, and a cow, or a horse. What do you think?"

"I'd love to have a horse. I wanna go riding more often," Linda said.

She looked down at the white baby chick and spoke to it again in a baby voice. She looked up for a moment, and then said, "I'll call him Alfred."

"Alfred? What if it's a chicken and not a rooster?"

Linda shrugged. "Too late now. He's Alfred. Do you think it's safe to leave him with the other chicks in the coop?"

"Why wouldn't it be?"

"Well, he's different. What if they hate him because of that?"

Jack laughed. "Chickens can't be racist, honey."

"Alright. I guess he needs to be with his brothers and sisters anyway. Okay, Alfred. Off you go."

Linda bent down and gently released Alfred into the coop. At first, the chick didn't move, but then it mingled with its friends. Linda took a step back and crossed her arms. When Jack looked at her, she had a fixed smile on her face. She noticed him staring, so she turned to kiss him and said, "I love our life."

"Me too, babe," Jack said.

"Let's have dinner, and then I'll give you your special present, birthday boy."

Chapter Twenty-Six

"Fuck," Jack said when the sputtering in the truck increased.

The roaring of the engine stopped, leaving the car in silent trundling on the dirt road. Not only that, but the truck's speed slowly decreased, and then no matter how many times Jack turned the key in the ignition, nothing happened.

The truck reached a halt, leaving Jack and the doctor in complete silence. Jack tried starting the car multiple more times, but to no avail. The entire time, the doctor patiently cast glances in Jack's direction.

"Guess we're walking," Jack finally said.

"You can't fix it?" William asked.

"I probably can, but it might take a while and I don't have the necessary tools. Come on, we're close to the farm anyway."

Jack opened the door and stepped outside into the cold air. William followed him out. Jack didn't like the idea of living his vehicle in the middle of the road to rust and possibly be swarmed by the undead, but right now, he had no choice.

William needed a moment to take a leak, and then the two of them walked down the path toward the farm. Jack looked at his truck one final time. He expected to feel sentimental about separating from the vehicle, but that feeling never came. Maybe with everything that happened, losing the truck seemed like an insignificant thing. If it happened before The Collapse, Jack wouldn't have been so indifferent, most likely.

The doctor and Jack were quiet throughout most of the walk. Jack actually enjoyed the walk. He had forgotten how peaceful the countryside could be. There was no traffic, no blaring horns of other impatient drivers, no swearing and yelling, no polluted air, and so on.

Maybe it was just an illusion for the moment, but Jack started to think that walks might be good for him. They were helping him clear his head and making him forget all about the problems on the farm. Cooped up inside the house and stuck with his own thoughts? That's when the problems manifested the most.

When they reached the meadow where the property was, Jack saw three undead roaming the landscape. They didn't attack Jack and William until they were relatively close. Jack took care of all three of them with the hatchet, leaving their bodies in the grass.

"Here we are, Doctor," Jack said as he stopped in front of the fence.

"This is your property?" William asked with a hint of skepticism in his tone.

"Yes. Don't worry, I didn't steal it from anyone or kill anyone to claim it for my own. I built it using my own money," Jack said.

"I'm sorry. I didn't mean it to sound that way."

"No offense taken."

Jack opened the gate and they went inside. As soon as the gate was safely locked again, Jack gestured for the doctor to continue toward the house. The doc seemed to be in a much better shape by then, and he no longer had the awkward walk like he did back on the highway.

"That was a close call. Thank you again, Jack," William said.

"Don't mention it. You must be hungry, huh?"

"I haven't eaten since yesterday morning."

"Feel free to sit wherever. I'll be back in a moment," Jack said.

He went to the pantry and retrieved two cans of beans. He hadn't even realized until then that he was starting to feel hungry himself.

"You like baked beans?" Jack shouted from the pantry.

"I like just about anything edible right about now!" William shouted back.

Jack returned to the living room to see the doctor sitting on the couch. He placed the cans of beans on the table and went into the kitchen to retrieve the spoons. By the time he returned, the doctor had already started eating with his fingers.

"Excuse my bad manners," he said.

"Don't worry about it." Jack slid the spoon to him.

They ate in silence. The doctor finished his can quickly, so Jack gave him an MRE packaged chicken sandwich. The thing looked disgusting, but the doctor ate it like it was a freshly cooked juicy burger. The entire time, Jack sneaked furtive glances at the doctor, trying to decipher what kind of a person he was.

"So, you said you used to be a doctor?" Jack asked as he dug through his baked beans.

The doctor nodded with his mouth full.

"Then you must know what's going on here. What's causing all this shit?" Jack asked.

William chewed his food slowly, and then gulped. He stared at the sandwich in his hand for a moment before raising his gaze to Jack. "I'm not an epidemiologist, but back before Eugene was overrun, my crew and I ran tests in the hospital lab."

"Okay?" Jack said, stuffing more beans into his mouth.

"We performed tests on infected humans without symptoms, as well as ones with symptoms. We also tested one who has died and resurrected as an undead."

"Sounds like you were thorough in your research."

"I wish. We didn't have the necessary equipment to conduct all the tests we wanted to, but we did discover interesting things about this virus."

"Virus?" Jack raised an eyebrow.

The doctor took a big bite of the sandwich and nodded. The side of his cheek bulged from the food in his mouth as he said, "Yes. This is all caused by a virus."

Jack swallowed his bite and focused on the doctor. As hungry as he was, he wanted to give his undivided attention to William's speech, because he felt like this would be crucial to finding a cure for Linda.

"We have no idea where it came from, but as always, there are rumors."

"What kind of rumors?"

"That the virus originated in Antarctica during the excavation of frozen marine life and accidentally spread to America, that it was government-created and there's been an accidental outbreak in the lab, that it is a bio-weapon used by China, and so on."

"What do you think is true?"

William swallowed. He stuffed the rest of the sandwich in his mouth, chewed for a few seconds, and then swallowed that, too. He looked at Jack, and then at the coffee table.

"It's impossible to say. I only know how it works. I don't know where it came from."

Scratching came from upstairs. William raised his eyebrows and looked at the ceiling. The scratching was slow and long, as if the person was dragging something sharp along the floor in steady motions. It repeated three times, and then it stopped.

"I thought you said you live alone," the doctor said.

"I did. I do. But um…" Jack pretended to chew to buy himself some time. "I've been having problems with mice lately."

"Mice?" William asked.

"Yeah. Is that going to be a problem for you?" Jack took another bite of his food.

"No problem at all. I would rather stay in here with mice than out there with… those things."

"Right. So, about the virus…"

William raised his hand to interrupt Jack. "If you don't mind, Jack. I would really like to get some sleep. I'm an old man, and I'm completely broken. I just need a few hours."

"Of course. No problem. You can sleep here on the couch if you like."

"Thank you. If I could repay you in any way, by working around the farm or anything like that…"

"Don't worry about it. Okay, I'm going to check upstairs to see if any of the mice got caught in the traps." Jack stood up.

The doctor nodded. He suddenly looked tired. He lay sideways and got ready to sleep. Jack climbed up the stairs and took one look down at the living room. The doctor's breathing was steady, and Jack wondered if he had already fallen asleep. He tip-toed up to the second floor and approached Linda's room.

He slowly pulled out the keys and inserted them into the keyhole. The lock clicked loudly when he turned it, reverberating throughout the entire corridor. Jack looked toward the stairs. He could hear the doctor's raspy breathing louder now. He was snoring.

Jack turned the knob and entered the room. Linda was staring out the window, her wheezing breaths synchronized with the doctor's snoring. Jack closed the door behind him – gently – and then turned to Linda. "Hey, babe," he whispered. "Sorry I left without a word earlier. Listen, I found a doctor. A doctor!" Jack couldn't contain his chuckle when he said that. "He's going to make you better, I just know it. But I need you to work with me, Linda. Don't make too much noise, okay?"

He looked over his shoulder at the door, as if that would help him check if the doctor had gotten up and was eavesdropping. He then faced Linda again. He almost jumped when he saw her facing him this time. She was still on the other side of the room, but he hadn't heard her when she spun around – not even a rattle of the chain.

"I know you're hungry, baby. But we're going to make you better. I'll tell the doctor about you, but I need time. I don't want to scare him. Okay?"

Linda, of course, didn't respond. She stared at Jack catatonically, her eyes fixated on him. Jack bit his lip. He turned around and exited the room without another word, and then locked it. The doctor's snoring came more prominently downstairs now.

With the house suddenly filled with sounds of another person sleeping, Jack himself became sleepy. He sauntered into the bedroom, slumped into bed, and closed his eyes. He remembered thinking that he should lock his bedroom door, just in case the doctor turned out to be a piece of shit like Nolan and Chris, but then he realized that he didn't really care that much.

Before he could entertain that thought properly, he drifted into another world.

****

He woke up to the sounds of rainfall. Jack glanced out the bedroom window and was greeted by a depressing hue of gray that stretched over the pane of glass like a blanket. He seriously started to hate the weather in Oregon.

Jack only then remembered the doctor, so he figured that he should check up on him, just in case. A pang of worry hit him at the thought that the doctor might have pilfered the pantry and taken off. The snoring that welcomed him once he stepped into the corridor told him that he had nothing to worry about.

Jack went to retrieve the radio from the kitchen and brought it upstairs, tip-toeing past William to avoid waking him up. The old man was splayed on the couch on his back, his mouth widely open, snoring so loudly that it almost sounded like sawing through a wooden board.

Once upstairs in the bedroom, Jack closed the door and turned on the radio. Gary's channel played music, as always. Jack lay in bed and listened, his mind focused on everything that had happened today. The doctor was knowledgeable about the outbreak, that much was obvious, but would he be able to help Linda?

Would he be willing *to help Linda?*

The hope Jack suddenly held onto like a drowning man was dangerous, he knew that much, but he couldn't let it go. It was his lifeline, and if that failed, he didn't know what he would do. He thought about the scenario where the doctor tells him that he can't help him, and that Jack has to go back to living his life with Linda like this.

Again, the shadow of doubt entered his mind momentarily. Should he spare Linda of this existence by ending her, or not lose hope on her? Just as quickly as those thoughts entered his mind, he pushed them out. He didn't like thinking about that. Whenever he did, he got a really bad feeling that he couldn't describe.

Gary's voice intervened to rescue Jack from his own head.

"This is Gary, and I'm talking to all the survivors out there," the radio man's voice perkily came from the speaker. "The horde is almost upon us. They will be here in less than a day. The Florence Eugene Highway will no longer be accessible, because the undead are all over it. Those of you who are in Eugene, pack your things and leave. It'll be at least a few hours until the entire horde passes."

A moment of pause ensued, and then Gary continued speaking.

"We've had reports in the past, from other stations, of people trying to be heroes and divert hordes in a different direction. If you're out there listening to this, do not risk your life to do that, because you're only going to make things worse. You'll only be splitting the horde into multiple little groups, and that way, they'll cover more area. Let them pass. Let the ones East of us deal with that problem."

The music resumed, but Jack couldn't help but linger on Gary's words. The ones East? Reports from other stations? It seems that there were way more survivors than Jack initially assumed. Small groups probably, but still groups of survivors. Jack wondered if they were planning to somehow clean the country of the undead, or if they were just… surviving. Probably the latter, because the undead vastly outnumbered the living.

Some time later, Jack turned off the radio and went downstairs. The doctor was awake by then, but looked like he didn't even know his own name. Jack decided to spare him the chit-chat and give him some time to properly wake up, so he went into the kitchen and sat there while listening to the rain.

William joined him a few minutes later, still looking comatose, but visibly more awake.

"You okay, Doctor?" Jack asked.

"I'm fine. I feel like I've just woken up from surgery." William rubbed his eyes.

"Well, you're free to get more sleep if you'd like."

"No, but thank you. I don't want to mess up my sleeping schedule."

Jack laughed when he realized that the doctor was serious. The world was falling apart, the living dead had decimated the civilization, and this doctor was worried about his body's natural clock.

"You can laugh, but it's very important," William said. "I'm an old man and I need to keep my immune system up. One night of not sleeping well and you suddenly have all these back aches, knee aches, joint problems, etcetera. You'll see when you get to my age."

"*If* I get to your age. You never know these days."

William seemed to realize that and regret his previous sentence because he opened his mouth slightly, but then looked down. For a moment, only the pitter-patter of the rain filled the kitchen. William leaned back in the chair, causing it to creak slightly. Jack couldn't help but worry that the chair would break under the doctor's weight, but he didn't want to say anything out of fear of offending him.

"They spoke on the radio earlier," Jack said. "The horde is headed straight for Eugene. And they mentioned that there are other survivors out there. There are probably way more of us than we initially thought."

"Hm," William frowned. "Have you thought about joining them?"

Jack hesitated. "This farm is pretty safe. And it's my home. I don't want to leave it."

"I see."

The doctor spoke atonally and calmly so far, exactly how a doctor would speak to a patient. It was difficult to tell what went on through his head. For all Jack knew, he could be plotting murder, and Jack would be none the wiser.

"Listen, I'd hate to bother you with more questions, but I want to know more about this virus," Jack said, abruptly changing the topic.

William leaned forward, the chair creaking again. He leaned his elbows on the table and intertwined his fingers. "You're really interested in this, aren't you?" he asked. "Very well. What would you like to know?"

"You said that you know how the virus works and all that. Tell me more about that." Jack felt his heart beginning to race, and he couldn't tell if it was excitement or dread that enveloped his body.

William cleared his throat. He now seemed almost fully awake. "As I said before, we don't know where it came from," he said. "Whatever it is, it's able to affect humans, obviously. The person infected displays symptoms similar to that of rabies – irritability, sensitivity to strong light that only further exacerbates their agitation, and limited cognitive abilities. Unlike the undead, who are driven by a strong urge for consumption of meat, the infected are driven to spread the virus. One bite is enough. That urge is so strong that the infected often put themselves in danger and suffer physical trauma. You must have seen it, right? Infected with broken arms and legs, or no arms and legs, attacking their prey regardless of their injuries?"

Jack nodded. He remembered the initial days of the outbreak when the infected were the dominant ones, and not the undead. It was a lot more chaotic, because the infected still retained their motor abilities and were far more dangerous than the undead.

"They feel no pain, or if they do, their urge for eating surpasses it," William continued. "The infected are still alive, but they are no longer in control of their own actions. The virus has taken over their body's functions, and they exist only as a vessel for the virus to spread the infection."

"Is the person who got infected still there, Doctor?" Jack asked.

He hadn't realized that he was leaning on the table and sitting at the edge of his seat, both figuratively and literally.

"Yes. But that person is no longer the same. The brain function deteriorates rapidly."

"Is there a cure?"

The doctor shook his head with lips pressed tightly. "Not that I know of. The CDC worked on developing a vaccine, but that takes a long time, and it only works in preventing the disease. It wouldn't cure the ones who already got it."

Jack leaned back in the chair. His mind swirled with the information the doctor had shared with him.

"There's no cure?" Jack asked.

"No. And with the governments no longer existing, we will never see one."

Jack felt his heart sink. Linda wasn't going to be cured. She was going to stay like this forever. That made him want to cry, but he suppressed the emotional wave in front of the doctor.

"What about the undead?" Jack finally asked, hazy.

"What about them?" William leaned back, causing another creak of the chair.

"The person who died and resurrected... are they still the same person?"

Jack's body trembled as if he had a fever. He almost didn't want to hear the answer to that, because he knew that what the doctor told him would shape everything he ever believed in. William ogled Jack for a moment, as if trying to read his face.

"Why do you want to know about that?" the doctor asked with concern in his voice.

On cue, the scratching upstairs started. This time, the doctor didn't look at the ceiling, but kept his gaze fixated on Jack instead. Jack thought he could detect fear in the old man. His eyes were slightly wider, and his shoulders seemed to tense up. His fists were closed as well.

"Sounds like a very serious mouse problem," William said with a calm voice.

Jack pushed his chair back as he stood up. "Come with me, Doctor. I want to show you something."

Chapter Twenty-Seven

He didn't expect to feel any different. They were husband and wife now, and he knew that their lives wouldn't change in any way except for the rings they would be wearing to indicate they were taken. And yet, when he put the ring on her finger and kissed her in front of all their family and friends, everything had changed.

Jack stared at himself in the mirror. The suit he wore didn't look good on him at all, he realized. He had tried adjusting it in different ways, but no matter what he did, he still looked bad in it. His best friend and best man Andrew convinced him that he looked fine, but Jack didn't agree.

Linda was probably going to look like a goddess in her wedding dress, and he wanted to hold up to standard, especially because her parents would be there, and Jack knew that they would be judging him every step of the way. They didn't actively disapprove of the wedding, but they didn't say anything good about it either, so Jack assumed that they were simply going with it despite not wanting their daughter to marry a farmer.

"Come on, you'll be fine, man," Andrew patted Jack on the back. "Listen, you could go out there wearing pajamas, and Linda would still think you look great. I've seen the way she looks at you, man. I think she likes you."

"I'm not sure if she likes me. I guess I'll ask her after the wedding," Jack sardonically said.

Andrew laughed. Someone knocked on the door, and Andrew had to go to take care of something, leaving

Jack alone in the room with his thoughts. Jack decided to give up on the adjustment of his suit and sat on the sofa, waiting for the time to pass.

With Andrew taking care of everything, the only thing Jack needed to do was to be present at the wedding. He appreciated that his friend did such an impeccable job as the best man. Andrew and Jack had known each other since early childhood. They went to the same daycare center, then to the same elementary, middle, and high school. By the time they finished high school, they continued hanging out almost on a daily basis.

When Jack first met Linda, and had doubts about what to do on a date, Andrew was there to offer him advice. Andrew was single, but Jack hoped that maybe tonight at the wedding, he would get lucky with one of the women.

A long time had passed with Jack sitting in silence in the room when Andrew returned and told him it was time. Jack's heart was hammering against his chest. Walking up to the altar was scary. Waiting in front of so many people with all their eyes fixed on him was terrifying. The nervousness of what was upcoming was debilitating.

All of that faded when Linda stepped into the room. Everything around her seemed to disappear when her eyes met with Jack's. She was the most beautiful woman in the room and in the world. Her white wedding dress radiated, or maybe it was Linda herself radiating the energy she brought in. Every step she took was slow, and Jack could hardly fight the urge to walk up to her instead.

When Linda's father finally walked her down the aisle, even he had a proud smile on his face. Standing in front of Linda, Jack felt as nervous as on their first date when they went rafting. She, on the other hand, entirely contrasted him. She had a smile on her face and didn't look nervous one bit. That gave Jack all the reassurance he needed.

Reading their vows was a blur to Jack. He had memorized his vow, but had to read off the paper because he was both so nerve-racked and mesmerized by Linda's beauty. He stuttered, and he knew that everyone in the room must have thought that he was an idiot, but he didn't care. He only cared about what Linda thought. She read her vow to him, and then they put the rings on each other's fingers.

Whenever he thought about wearing the wedding ring, Jack thought of it as a burden. But as the ring slid down his finger, he felt the bond between him and Linda only further strengthening. She was now and forever officially his, and he was hers.

When the officiant told them that they may kiss, Jack's legs became wobbly, but in a good way. No other woman could cause him to feel that way. As their lips met, Jack became aware of one thing.

He wanted nothing more than to spend the rest of his life and beyond with Linda.

Chapter Twenty-Eight

"Don't worry, Doctor. I'm not going to butcher you so I can eat you," Jack said when he climbed up the stairs and looked down at the doctor.

William had a slightly concerned look on his face. Jack could tell that he really did think that Jack was preparing a trap for him.

"Doctor, if I wanted to kill you, I would have done it while you were sleeping," Jack said, now slightly impatient.

That seemed to convince William, because he nodded and climbed the stairs. Jack stopped in front of Linda's room. He waited for the doctor to approach him, and then he pulled out the keys.

"My wife trusted the wrong people," Jack said as he inserted the key. "She was trying to help them, but they ended up killing her."

"I'm so sorry to hear that."

Jack turned the key. The lock resounded in an obnoxiously loud manner. "Don't be. She was a good person. Didn't have a bad bone in her body." He pulled the key out and put it in his pocket. "I need your help, Doctor. You know more about this disease than I do."

Jack pushed the door open, revealing the interior of the room. He took a step back, silently gesturing William to go inside. The doctor was visibly unnerved now. His body was tense, and he retained a focused stare. He peeked inside the room. A loud growl and rattle of the chain resounded, and the doctor recoiled, hitting his back against the corridor's wall with a yelp.

"What in the–" William uttered.

"It's okay! She can't hurt you!" Jack raised his palms to intervene before the doctor ran away in panic. "I had her tied up."

"What in the world is the meaning of this?!" William asked, intermittently darting from Jack to Linda.

Linda's chain was taut as she strained to reach the new person she had never seen before. She clawed at the air in futility, trying to grab the doctor, not getting close by a dozen feet.

"It's my wife, Linda," Jack calmly said.

"No! This thing's a monster! What the hell were you thinking?! Do you wanna get yourself killed?!"

Jack frowned. He suddenly became angry. "That's my wife you're talking about!" he shouted.

William realized the harshness of his words, because he gave Jack a momentary solicitous glance. He was no longer pressed against the wall for dear life, but he did keep his eyes on Linda. He looked at Jack, then at Linda, and then back at Jack.

"When did your wife die?" he asked.

"A few months ago."

"You've kept her in this room for months?"

"What did you expect me to do? Kill her?"

"Yes! That's exactly what you should have done, Jack!"

Jack pressed his lips tightly. He didn't like where this conversation was headed. He shrugged and said, "Doc, please. You're my last hope for this. Please, help me cure my wife. She's all I've got. Please." Tears blurred his vision, but he blinked them away.

"I'm willing to tell you everything I know, but not here. Downstairs," William said. His gaze was still fixated on Linda. He looked like he expected the chain holding her in place to snap at any moment.

Jack looked at Linda. She hadn't ceased her clawing and growling for a moment since she first saw the doctor. "Okay," Jack said and closed the door. The growling continued, albeit muffled. Jack locked the door and gestured toward the stairs.

He and the doc climbed down. Jack's head was spinning. The doctor now knew about Linda, and he didn't run away. That was good. That meant that they'd be able to talk normally. They sat in the living room and spent a long moment in silence. The wall clock ticked with each passing second, slightly alleviating the awkward stillness in the air.

"Your wife is an undead," William finally spoke, breaking the silence.

"Yes." Jack nodded.

"I thought you said she trusted the wrong kind of people."

"She did. And they shot her. When I held her in my arms, and when I saw her dying… I felt myself dying, too." Jack suddenly saw flashing images of Linda shot and bleeding on the living room floor. "I couldn't lose her. I was so afraid of losing her, Doctor."

His voice trembled at the final sentence, and he fought the urge to break down. He had to tell his story to the doctor. Maybe that way the old man might feel some sympathy.

"She wasn't going to survive the wound. The undead were on the farm. I lured one inside and had him bite Linda, so that she would get infected and rise after dying. I left her inside the room, and in the morning… she was alive again."

Jack let out a meager peal of laughter even though nothing was funny. It felt oddly weird, but also good to talk about it. It was also scary, because now that he spoke about it, it felt all the more real, and he felt a bevy of emotions that he had buried deep creeping up from the darkest pits of his soul. The doctor stared at him unblinking, with a serious facial expression.

"Please, William. Please tell me there's something I can do to save her. Please." The tears that had formed in Jack's eyes now freely slid down his cheeks.

"Jack," the doctor said, somewhat stern in his tone, "There is no cure."

Jack inhaled sharply, and then sighed. He already knew that. Of course, he knew it. He just held onto the hope that there would be a miraculous cure to save his wife. Jack buried his face in his hands and wept.

"I'm sorry, Jack. The best thing you can do is put her out of her misery and move on with your life."

"I can't. She's my wife, I can't kill her!" Jack sobbed.

"Jack, listen to me," William said, like a teacher who was about to give his student a valuable piece of advice. "That thing up there is no longer your wife."

That thing, the words reverberated in Jack's skull like a ball getting ping-ponged back and forth. Jack stopped sobbing and looked at the doctor. "Wh… what are you talking about?"

The doctor shifted slightly in his seat. "I told you that we performed tests. When the person gets infected, they are still alive, but their brain function very quickly deteriorates."

"You already said so."

"But when the infected person dies, the virus brings them back to life. Or so that's what it looks like."

Jack sat ramrod straight to listen to the doctor. He knew that every piece of information was important.

"Go on," Jack said as he wiped his tears.

William cleared his throat. "We thought that the virus reanimates the person, but it doesn't do that. What it does instead is it reactivates the dead body and controls it. We performed thorough tests, and we now know that the undead are not actually undead. They are really just walking corpses controlled by the virus like puppets."

"N-no. That can't be. I mean..." Jack tried to string words together to form a coherent sentence, but it didn't work.

"The person is gone once they die," William confirmed. "We have tested it many times over and I can confirm that the person upstairs is not your wife anymore. It's a virus controlling her body."

Jack stared at the coffee table for a long moment. He felt numb. William must have sensed that because he gave him time to digest everything.

"They're no longer human?" Jack finally asked with a cracked voice as he looked at William.

"I'm afraid not."

Jack sighed again. He didn't want to believe the doctor. It all sounded like bullshit. It made him angry at William. For a moment when he looked at him, he thought about how easy it would be to kill him right here, right now. He could get his gun, shoot him in the head, and feed him to Linda. Pretend he never met the doctor. Pretend the conversation in the living room never took place. It would be that simple.

His gaze gravitated back to the coffee table. He suddenly felt ashamed of his thoughts. He started sobbing again. He heard the doctor's footsteps as they approached him, and then felt a firm reassuring hand on his shoulder.

It was exactly what Jack needed. He wanted his Linda back, and he knew that he was never going to get her. That realization hurt like a thousand knives getting twisted in his heart. He cried even harder, and he cried even when he thought he could no longer cry.

He cried until the world faded into nothingness.

Chapter Twenty-Nine

When Jack opened his eyes, the coffee table greeted his vision. He blinked, the remnants of his sadness from the earlier fit still pervading his mind and body. Jack wanted to die. The ticking of the clock reverberated loudly in Jack's skull. The pattering of the rain had stopped, he noticed.

He got into a sitting position and rubbed his eyes. The house was quiet. Jack called out to William, but there was no response. He stood up with a groan and dragged himself toward the front door, feeling like he was lugging three dead bodies on his shoulders. He opened the door and glanced at the gloomy sky.

He heard crackling coming from somewhere on the property. He recognized the sound as fire. Immediately, the noise was accompanied by a pleasant smell. Something was cooking, but Jack couldn't tell what. Jack went down the porch and walked around the house. The smell became more prominent, and Jack's brain registered what it was the moment he ran into William.

The old man sat on an old chair in front of a campfire. The fire crackled, and above it, William held a pan with a pancake cooking inside. Next to him was a basket of blueberries.

"What are you doing?" Jack asked with a raspy voice.

"Making pancakes," William said matter-of-factly as he scooped up the pancake with a spatula in his free hand and flipped it. The pancake sizzled when it dropped into the pan.

Then Jack saw other things around William. A few pieces of firewood, a container full of pancake mixture, and a tray with already finished blueberry pancakes.

"Where'd you get the blueberries?" Jack asked.

"Went out into the woods earlier. You know, you have enough food in the woods around you to last you a long time. You know how to set up snares and traps?"

"I don't."

"Me neither. Too bad, because I see a lot of animals around here. Here, try one of these." William bent down and picked up the tray. He handed it to Jack, but Jack only took one pancake from the stack.

Jack took a bite where he saw a blueberry protruding. The taste was heavenly. Not only did Jack finally bite into something warm, but he had forgotten how damn tasty pancakes were – or maybe it was just William's recipe that made them taste so good. He wondered if the undead felt the same when they bit into the flesh of the living. That image didn't dissuade him from continuing to eat the pancake.

"Damn. These are good." Jack nodded.

"Some syrup on them would have been nicer, but it doesn't matter," William said as he overturned the pan above the tray, causing the cooked pancake to flop on top of the stack. He then put the tray down, added a piece of firewood into the fire, and poured the pancake mixture into the pan before sprinkling a handful of blueberries on top.

"Used to make these for my grandchildren all the time," William said.

Jack opened his mouth to ask him about his grandchildren, but he then realized that maybe it was better not to do so. Jack ate the whole pancake, and once William cooked the entire batch, they put out the fire and went inside to eat. Their spirits were high because of the meal they had, and William even became talkative about things other than the virus and the outbreak.

He told Jack how he worked as a GP in Eugene, and how many people thought he was the grumpiest doctor ever. Jack remembered hearing stories about him – people talked about the old doctor as being so rough with the patients, that even if they came to his office healthy, they left in a bad shape. Those were exaggerated stories among the older generations of course, and in reality, William was a respectable doctor who often attended conferences, seminars, and webinars.

The old man didn't talk about his family, and Jack didn't want to be pushy about it. Whatever happened to them must not have been good because it was visible that the doctor skirted around the topic. The scratching upstairs killed the mood in the room. It was already dark outside by then, and William said that he would prefer to sleep now because he was tired.

Jack didn't argue with him about that. Jack was feeling tired as well, so he went upstairs. He checked on Linda once more. She was calm, but Jack worried that she might be starving and not showing it. He wished her goodnight before dragging himself to bed.

He fell asleep almost immediately.

****

A muffled jovial voice downstairs snapped him out of his dreamless sleep. Jack opened his eyes wide and

219

listened. It was still dark. The voice spoke fast and without taking long breaks to inhale. It took him a moment to realize that the voice belonged to Gary from the radio. William must have been listening to it.

Jack was thirsty, so he threw the blankets off him and stood up. It was cold, and he didn't feel like leaving the warmth of his bed, but he was parched from the pancakes. As soon as he opened the door, the voice on the radio crystalized.

"Bad news folks, bad fuckin' news," Gary said. "It would seem that the horde is separating. While the majority is headed for Eugene, we can see a huge number of them breaking off and heading South. We know that there are some properties in the way, so if you're the owner of said properties, get the hell out of there."

Jack frowned. South? Jack's farm was South. He walked downstairs to find William sitting on the couch, intently focused on the radio on the table.

"I repeat, folks. The horde is headed for Eugene, but a bunch of them have separated and are going South down the dirt road. If you're either in Eugene or in the properties South, get out of there. You have only two hours left. Now is also the time for us to reveal where you guys can stay. We've worked really hard to create a sanctuary for everyone. We are located in Cloverdale, just East of the Emerald Valley Golf Club, South of Eugene. Everybody who needs shelter, come to Cloverdale. We have electricity. We have food and water. We have weapons. We have walls. Most importantly, we have people who want to rebuild America. We are unstoppable here."

William and Jack exchanged glances. Cloverdale. They set up a community there. It meant that it would be safe from the undead. Gary continued repeating the information about the horde and Cloverdale.

"The horde going South. They're going to run straight into the farm," Jack said in a low voice as he sat into the sofa across from William. "I don't understand. Why would the horde break off like that?"

William looked at him with a forlorn grimace. "They do that sometimes. They catch a scent or see something interesting, they start following it, and the ones behind follow them without knowing what's going on. Either way, it's too dangerous to stay on the farm."

Jack bit his lip. "I can't leave," he said.

"If you stay here, you will be overrun. The fence won't hold. You heard Gary. They have a safe place in Cloverdale."

"Are you going to head there?"

"Yes. I think I will. I'm tired of living like this. I can't keep dreading if I'm going to wake up to see an undead biting my leg, or a raider pickpocketing me. They'll need a doctor over there. I want to see if I can help other people in need."

Jack nodded. "Then let me help you pack supplies before you leave." He smiled.

"Jack, you're seriously going to stay here?"

"Yes."

"You can't possibly think that–"

"I have a wife, Doctor. I'm not just going to leave her. I've already made up my mind. Don't try to talk me out of it."

Jack and the doctor stared at each other for a moment. The old man must have seen the determination on Jack's face, because a moment later, he nodded. Jack felt bad about letting the doctor go out there defenseless, so he gave him a handgun and some bullets. He also packed a bunch of food and water for him in a backpack. The entire time, William hadn't tried to persuade Jack to go with him, and Jack was grateful for that.

"Thank you for all your help, Jack," William said when they went outside on the porch. The rain had already stopped by then, leaving a dreary gray sky. "I would have been dead if you hadn't saved me on the highway."

"Don't mention it."

"I'm sorry that we have to depart on such terms. It's not too late, Jack. You can still come with me. They'll need farmers in Cloverdale, I'm sure of it."

"I can't. I have to take care of my wife."

William flashed him a smile for the first time today. It looked unnatural on the old man.

"You know, my family died when all this started," he said. "Every single one of them. My wife, my daughters, my grandchildren. All of them perished before I could even say goodbye. For a long time, I wondered if continuing to live was even worth it. But then I ran into a family. They had no food, and their five-year-old son was sick. I used my skills as a doctor to help him recover. I had no hopes that he would live long. Not in this world. But when I saw how happy his parents were when he was able to start walking again… it was priceless. That's what we're still fighting for, Jack. Those fleeting moments of happiness. My family has died, but I want to help others avoid the same fate. I firmly believe that my purpose in life is to help others who are in need."

Jack smiled. "Well, never too late to find a new hobby, I suppose," he said.

"No need for sarcasm, Jack. I want you to think about what I said. That's all. And if you change your mind and come to Cloverdale, free checkups for a lifetime. My lifetime, not yours.”

Both Jack and William laughed at that. “I will think about it. Thanks, Doc.”

William nodded and turned to walk down the porch.

“Doctor, wait,” Jack called out.

William turned around. Jack tossed him the car keys. The doctor clumsily grabbed them with a jingle, and then looked at Jack.

“Cloverdale is not so close. Use the car out back. But be careful, because it used to belong to the raiders,” Jack said.

“What about you? You still need wheels if you’re going to go on supply runs.”

“I think I prefer walking now.”

William nodded. Jack opened the fence for him and waited until he drove out. William waved from the car’s interior, and then stepped on the gas pedal and drove down the meadow. Jack waved back, and then closed the fence and locked it. No undead were out in the meadow, but he didn’t want to risk them breaking in before the horde arrived.

Jack looked at the dirt road from which he expected the undead horde to emerge. He didn’t have a lot of time, he knew that much. Night had already started falling, and he assumed that he would hear them before he saw them. Gary said that they had a couple of hours tops, and that was not nearly enough time to prepare a good defense.

No defenses would stop the oncoming horde. Jack couldn’t be sure how big the horde was going to be, but if Gary said that they should get out of the way, then it had to be big. Jack should have laid more traps in front of the property when he had the chance.

Too late for that now.

A tapping from the window above snapped him out of his thoughts. He looked up. Although he couldn't see her, he knew that the tapping came from Linda.

"I'm coming home, Linda," Jack said as he walked back inside the house.

Chapter Thirty

"The horde has just entered Eugene, folks. There's so many of them, I don't think I've ever seen so many people bunched up together. If you're for some reason still stuck in Eugene, find a safe place to hide and stay still and quiet until this whole thing blows over. If you're on the streets and you have nowhere to hide, run. Run and don't stop until you can longer see any of those undead bastards anymore."

The music had stopped long ago, and Gary spoke, no longer calmly and coherently, but rapidly and with a concerned timbre. Jack listened as he took all the important items he had and placed them on the table of the living room one by one. Food, water, weapons and bullets, meds, clothes, backpack, rope, hatchet, flashlight, fork, kitchen utensils, the radio, batteries.

"We don't know where the horde will go after Eugene," Gary said. "They might continue East, but it's possible that they might split into smaller groups and go in different directions. Either way, we'll keep a lookout and inform you of any changes."

Jack stared at the items splayed on the table. He'd been hoarding so many of them, but now he would need to get rid of most of them because they wouldn't fit in his backpack. Water and food were the most important, so he decided to pack those at the top of the backpack.

He first packed a pair of socks, pants, sweater, undershirt, underpants, and sneakers, squeezing the clothes at the bottom of the backpack as much as he could, to save as much as space as possible. He then packed water bottles and cans of food – mostly focusing on the food he personally liked. He placed the meds into the side pockets of the backpack, as well as the utensils and the batteries, and some bullets. He put most of the bullets in his jacket, to always have them close by.

He slid the hatchet into the compartment strap and tied it up so that it held firm. By the time he zipped up his backpack, it was bulging with the items he had inside. It was pretty heavy, too. Jack had hoisted it on his back to see what it felt like. The straps were a little short, so he loosened them just a bit, because he still wanted the backpack to remain firmly on his back.

Some of the weapons he had would need to be relinquished. Jack had a handgun in his back pocket, but he still had one handgun and one assault rifle on the table. He opted to keep the handgun in his pocket because it was compatible with most of the ammunition he had.

"The smaller horde headed South is not stopping, folks," Gary said. "There are stragglers breaking off from the main group and getting lost in the woods, but the main group is like a truck. It's going to be impossible to go anywhere near those woods for a while, folks. I think this is the end of Eugene and the surrounding areas as we know it."

Jack went from room to room, scrutinizing every object to see if there was anything else he needed to get off the farm before the horde hit it. Every object here was tied to a memory of him and Linda, and he wished that he didn't need to choose, because he suddenly felt attached to every decoration, every piece of furniture, every book, every glass, every electronic item.

Wherever he looked, he saw Linda. He could still see her smiling from the couch as she read a book aloud to Alfred, who would be sitting next to her. He could still hear her soft voice as it changed when she read and when she spoke to Jack. He could still see her in the kitchen, wearing an apron and oversized mittens while making cupcakes and muffins, flour covering her nose or cheeks.

He could still see her in the bedroom posing in a new dress in front of the mirror, asking Jack if he liked it. He liked everything on her, of course, but she seemed to wear things specifically because Jack liked them on her. He could still see her in bed, sleeping on the side with the hair in her face, her shoulder slowly rising and falling.

He could still feel the warmth of her body as she pressed against him when they were naked in bed during a cold night. He could still feel her long hair tickling his face as she leaned to kiss him. He could still feel the electricity surging through his body when their lips touched.

Jack felt an immense heartache. He went outside the house and made a lap around it. The night was still, and the insects were loudly chirping. Jack wondered for a moment what it was like being an insect in a zombie apocalypse. Did they know what it was like living in such a world? Did they even care?

For a moment, Jack lingered in front of the chicken coop. The day he brought the baby chicks home entered his mind. Linda's excitement as she saw the chicks and named Alfred.

I'd love to have a horse. I wanna go riding more often.

Jack never got her that horse. He planned on surprising her with it for her next birthday, but then The Collapse happened and everything went to hell. Jack gently put a hand on the fence of the chicken coop. He couldn't help but feel like the outcome of all this could have been so much different.

The words of Linda's father invaded his head – how he judged Jack for wanting to take his daughter and live on the farm. *It looks like he was right about everything.* No, that was a stupid way to think. The ones living in the cities were probably all dead, including Jack's and Linda's parents. Jack wondered for a moment what would Grant do to Jack if he found out his daughter was now an undead. Jack felt like puking at that thought, so he quickly dismissed it and stepped away from the chicken coop.

He went around the back of the house where his eyes once again fell on the damaged fence. The mesh still held sturdy, and Jack just then remembered that he hadn't done regular patrols around the fence in a while. In the end, it didn't even matter because in a matter of hours, the entire farm was going to get bulldozed by the horde.

Jack had seen the horde in action before. They didn't knock walls of buildings down, but they did go through doors and windows, and tore down flimsy fences. He'd seen the ones at the front pressed up against the closed door, only to get squished under the weight of their peers pushing from behind.

The same would happen at the farm when the horde reached the fence. They wouldn't go around it, but would press against it until it slanted. The ones at the front would get sliced at the mesh wire, but the fence would fall, and the horde would go through the door, and eventually come out the back and destroy the backside of the fence, too.

Ten minutes had already gone by since Jack went outside. He was without a jacket, and it was cold. He looked in the direction where William drove off just twenty minutes ago. He wondered if the old man would be okay. With that thought, he strode back inside the house. Gary's voice still filled the air of the house, but this time, it didn't alleviate Jack's loneliness.

"–thing about this is that the raiders from Eugene are going to get flushed out. They'll have no place to hide anymore. We know who they are, and if they come in our direction, we'll give them swift retribution for all the lives they took. On another note–"

Jack pressed the button to turn off the radio. The room fell deafeningly silent. Jack could hear his own quavering breathing for the first time in many hours. He suddenly felt cold all over his body, and he was sure that it wasn't from the temperature outside. Jack stared at the bulging backpack, the flashlight, the radio, and the guns on the table. So many important things packed into such condensed space – and none of those things were of sentimental value, only supplies that would allow him to survive.

He and Linda spent hours transporting things of personal value to them to the farm, and now Jack would be leaving all of them behind to be swept in the wave of the undead or left to collect dust and rot.

Shuffling noise came from above, as if on cue. Linda could tell that something was going on, Jack thought. He looked at the ceiling, feeling his face growing warm from an oncoming wave of tears. He sniffled and exhaled slowly with his eyes closed.

He grabbed the flashlight and walked upstairs.

Chapter Thirty-One

The door creaked open. The flashlight in Jack's hand brightly illuminated the room, and Linda in it. The pale light made her look even more sickly than she was. Linda faced Jack and was as still as ever.

"Hi, babe," Jack said with a smile.

She didn't smile back, of course. Jack stepped inside and his eyes fell on *The Witch of the Woods* on the mattress. The book remained untouched, just as he had left it. Linda followed Jack with her gaze, her wheezy breaths filling the room. Jack closed the door behind him.

He sauntered to the mattress and grabbed the book from it. He felt Linda's gaze on him. Jack walked to the chair and sat on it. He spent a moment ogling Linda, and then looked down at the book.

"I never understood why you liked this book," he said. "It's a nice fairy tale, I get that. But I've read better ones. I suppose you had a connection with Will and Zara, huh? I'm Will, and you're Zara, and the book shows what lengths you'd go to in order to save me from the evil witch. I have no doubt that if the roles were reversed, and I were stuck in this room, you would have traveled the country on foot all the way to the East coast and back, just to find a way to bring me back."

Jack chuckled forlornly. "Or maybe you'd spare me of such an existence and put a bullet in my head immediately. That's definitely what I would want you to do to me. And I know you wanted the same. You didn't want to live like this." He bent down and placed the book on the floor. He then leaned back in the chair again and smiled.

"You remember our first date?" he asked with warm reminiscence. "I was so nervous. I'd never been so nervous for a date before. I guess I knew even then that you were the right one, and it probably scared me to lose you before we even fell in love. I thought I was so smart when I chose rafting as our date activity. And then I felt so stupid when we missed the turn and got carried by the current."

Jack chuckled heartily at the memory of him and Linda holding onto the raft for dear life while the water splashed inside from all sides. "You were completely soaked and freezing, and I thought that I had lost my chance for a second date. But I still remember it like it was yesterday. The way you taught me about the plants there. I didn't even care about botany, but when I heard you talking about it, it suddenly made me want to become a scientist."

Another peal of bittersweet laugh left Jack's mouth. Linda stared at him blankly, not giving any indication that she understood a word. A part of Jack hoped that she would, because he desperately needed something that would tell him that William was wrong, and that holding onto the meager hope Jack had was not a mistake.

"But then when we sat at the campfire, I felt so irresistibly attracted to you. I had to get close to you, even just a little, but no matter how close I got, it wasn't enough. And when we kissed…" Jack looked down for a moment. "The entire day after that, I couldn't tell if I was dreaming or not. Whenever I closed my eyes, I saw your face, and it was the most beautiful face in the world. It still is."

He gave Linda another heartfelt smile, but she didn't reciprocate it. All she ever did was stare at him. Jack sighed. "God, what am I even saying? You don't understand a word! You're not you! You're not Linda! You're just..." He gestured fervently toward Linda while raising his tone. He couldn't find the word to finish that sentence. His hand drooped and he exhaled a shallow breath.

"The doctor couldn't help you. I'm sorry, Linda. I asked him, but... there's no cure. He can't bring you back. I guess I've been fooling myself all this time. I thought that we could live a normal life like this. That you would remember me one day and things would go back to the way they were before you..."

Jack felt tears forming in his eyes. He squeezed his eyes shut, and the tears slid down his cheeks. "There's something important I need to talk to you about, Linda. There's a horde coming straight toward the farm. The property won't survive. Everything we built here is going to be gone in just a matter of hours. I could let you bite me. Just one nibble, and we'd be together forever, even in death. I would like nothing more."

He looked down at his hand and imagined Linda biting off one finger. He wondered what it felt like getting infected. Would he be aware of everything? He would finally be able to see the world through Linda's eyes after dying. He looked at Linda again.

"There's a second option. There's a group of survivors in Cloverdale. They claim they have a very strong camp there. It's Gary from the radio. You remember him, babe? They're no longer in Eugene's cathedral. I want us to go there, but I'm afraid that if we go, they'll shoot us both on sight. Best case scenario, they would let only me inside while leaving you out – provided you didn't kill me before that. I could never leave you out there alone in the world while I'm safe inside the walls with other survivors." He sniffled and wiped the tears off his face.

"There's also a third and final option, but I don't like it. I think… I think the reason why I don't like it is because I know it's the only right one. You made me promise to put you down if you ever got infected. And you wanted me to continue fighting. But Linda, I don't see the point of going on if you're not here with me." His voice cracked toward the end, but he cleared his throat and refused to allow another sobbing fit to start. "I have to fulfill my promise to you. It was your final wish. I don't know if I'll be strong enough to survive without you, but I'll try, because it's what you wanted."

The tears now freely flowed down his face. Jack stood up and withdrew the handgun from his pocket. Linda continued staring at him, oblivious to what was going on. Jack removed the safety on the gun with trembling hands.

"I love you, Linda. I'll always love you. I know you're watching me right now. Maybe not from your physical body, but I know you're watching me and protecting me. It's the only reason I stayed alive for so long."

He raised his hand and pointed the gun at Linda's head. Immediately, Linda started moving. She took a step forward and outstretched her arms toward Jack. She bared her teeth at Jack, gnashing and snapping. She growled and hissed at Jack, desperately wanting to get a bite out of him, the chain stopping her in place.

As Jack stared at her, he couldn't help but see a person who was no longer his wife. It was as if the veil had been lifted, and he saw not Linda, but someone else behind those eyes. No, the veil had never been here. He was just too blind to see the truth.

Jack put his finger on the trigger and whimpered. His finger trembled on the metal, just as his entire hand did. Linda's forehead was aligned within the crosshairs of the gun, mere inches from her. She didn't seem to care that the deadly black barrel was staring at her. She just wanted food, and only food. Jack turned his head away and closed his eyes, tears coming out of his eyes in waves. He tried really hard to imagine Linda watching him from somewhere in Heaven, holding a hand on his shoulder, and telling him that everything was going to be alright.

Before Jack could change his mind, he squeezed the trigger.

Chapter Thirty-Two

She was his light in a tunnel full of darkness. With her by his side, he could conquer the world. Without her, he stumbled blindly through the pitch black, alone and scared.

"I don't care if all the undead in the world come down on us. I will always protect you, Linda," Jack said.

He and Linda were lying in bed, facing each other. It was dark, but Jack could see Linda's face clearly. She smiled at him. Her fingers gently brushed his cheek. She leaned forward and gave him a kiss on the nose.

"I know," she said. "I know you'd never let anything bad happen to me. I think the only person who needs assurance of that is you, Jack."

Jack gulped.

"I have always believed in you and your decisions, babe, no matter what other people said" Linda continued. "Even when you didn't see your own value, I saw it. Ever since the first day when you walked into my work, I knew you had something special in you."

That evoked a smile out of Jack. He put a hand over Linda's on his cheek. His mind wandered toward the nasty scenarios of what might happen in the future. He suddenly envisioned himself living on the farm alone. The thought of waking up alone in bed, doing his daily activities without Linda's voice to fill the house, and then going to bed alone, terrified Jack beyond words. A tight knot formed in his stomach.

"Linda, if anything happens, I just want you to know that I love you very much," he said.

"I know. I love you too, Jack. If something were to happen to me tomorrow or whenever, I want you to know that I will never stop loving you, no matter what the circumstances of our departure were. I know how easily you can feel guilty about things, so I want you to remember that there's nothing that could jeopardize my love for you."

Jack bit his lip, suppressing the uncomfortable feeling climbing up toward his face.

"No matter what you see out there, I want you to keep fighting. Alright?" Linda asked.

Jack could muster only a feeble nod. He really didn't want to have this conversation, even though he knew that the chances of something happening to either of them was a big possibility. "And one more thing," Linda added.

"What?"

"Take care of Alfred for me." She smiled.

Epilogue

Jack barely registered the loud gunshot that reverberated in the room and caused his ears to ring. He only registered that Linda's growling had stopped. Silence gradually filled the room, and Jack willed himself to lower his hand and open his eyes.

At first, he refused to look at the floor. But then his head inadvertently turned, and he saw her. She was on her back, a red hole in her forehead, her eyes open. There was no blood on the floor. Jack realized what he had done, and that caused him to drop his gun on the ground.

He let out a wail and collapsed on his knees. He took Linda into his arms and cried loudly while hugging her tightly. She was ice-cold, but he didn't care. He felt something that he should have felt that fateful night when she got shot, so long ago. He couldn't describe the feeling as anything more than loss.

Jack felt as if he had just lost the best part of him, the part of him that he lived and breathed for. The sharp pain in his heart was out of this world, and he wished more than anything to follow Linda wherever she had gone. Jack squeezed Linda feverishly in his arms, afraid that her body would somehow disappear out of his tight hug. He couldn't lose her body, he just couldn't. It was the only thing he had left of her.

He couldn't tell how long had passed with him holding Linda and rocking back and forth in the pale cone of the flashlight. He only knew that the tears in his eyes had dried out, and he felt utterly broken. He knew that he couldn't stay here, but he also couldn't leave Linda in the house to rot.

Jack gently placed Linda's hands on her chest, kissed her forehead with trembling lips, and stood up. The stench in the room was no longer unpleasant. Jack wanted to close the door to stop the air from wafting out, because it was the air Linda breathed, and he didn't want it gone. He took the flashlight and the gun and went outside. He went around the back of the house and grabbed a shovel. He then started digging next to the chicken coop.

The night was cold, but he didn't care. He didn't feel the chill at all. The more he dug, the less he felt it. He was pretty quick at work and before he knew it, he was standing in a three-foot deep hole, his hands slightly calloused from the aggressive shoveling.

Once he was done, he threw the shovel out and jumped out of the hole. He wiped the bead of sweat off his forehead. He was tired, which was great, because it kept the feeling of despair away. That feeling would come later, and he would deal with it then.

Jack went back to Linda, gently wrapped her in a blanket, and carried her outside. He hadn't felt the feeling of loss creeping up on him again until he placed her in the grave. Jack ran back upstairs and grabbed *The Witch of the Woods*. By the time he returned with the book to Linda in the grave, he was shaking all over and barely had the strength to speak.

"Here, baby. Take this," he said as he placed the book on her chest. "It's your favorite book." He shuddered and gasped violently. He then took her hand into his and took her wedding ring off. It took some effort to have it come off because of Linda's bloated skin and the crusted blood.

Jack looked at the ring. Although blood made it difficult to see, the words on the interior of the rim were visible.

My love for you is eternal.

Jack broke down again. He felt like his heart was going to burst from the pain he felt, and he hoped that it would. He just wanted all this to be over. Why didn't he do this months ago when Linda first died? He now would have been past the initial stage of grieving. He collapsed sideways and remained on the cold ground in a fetal position for a long time, sobbing and wailing.

When he finally stopped, he put Linda's wedding ring on his ring finger, so that he had both his and her ring on his finger. The rings would never come off, even after he died, he decided.

Jack got closer to Linda and gave her one final, long kiss on the forehead. He almost regretted it, because it made it harder for him to separate from her. He wanted to stay with her forever, buried together in that pit. But that would be breaking his promise to her again.

Jack stood up, tucked Linda into the blanket and grabbed the shovel. With each shovel of dirt that he tossed into the grave, his heart grew heavier, but he had to keep going. He threw the dirt in a way that he covered her body first, and only then moved onto tossing the dirt on the blanketed head.

By the time Jack finished, he was exhausted, but the ground was covered. He patted the dirt with the flat side of the shovel, and now it almost looked like the ground had never been dug out in the first place. Linda would be safe there from the horde in here. And from everything else. Jack wanted to make a cross for Linda, but it would probably only get trampled by those fuckers, so he decided to leave it like this.

Jack leaned the shovel against the wall and took one full jerry can. He went inside the house and climbed upstairs. He went from room to room and poured gasoline all over the walls, the furniture, and the floor. He then went downstairs and did the same. One can was not enough, so he grabbed another one and repeated the process until the entire house smelled like gasoline.

He took the radio into one hand went out through the front door. He placed the radio on the ground, opened the fence, and that's when he heard it. The moans of the undead were upon him – distant, but getting closer with each passing second.

Turning around, Jack saw a bunch of figures clustered together at the far end of the road. They indeed looked like an army from here because of the sheer numbers. Just from what he could see, there must have been at least a thousand of them, but Jack assumed that there were way more behind.

Jack took out his lighter and flicked it on. The flame sparked to life, the only glowing thing in the dark night. He brought the flame to the gasoline-soaked porch and let it catch. The flame whooshed on the wood, and quickly spread into the house.

Very quickly, the interior of the house caught on abundant waves of fire, illuminating the entire property and igniting it with heat that kept Jack uncomfortably warm. The moans of the undead grew louder, but Jack knew that the flaming house would keep them occupied, giving him the chance to slip away.

Something crashed inside the house. The flames licked the walls and crackled in the silence of the night, but that serenity was interrupted by the ever-growing sounds of the undead.

Jack turned his head to face Linda's grave. He hoisted his backpack by the strap higher on his shoulder and turned to walk through the fence, the radio in his hand. The undead were focused on the burning house now. They would head straight into it, not caring that they would burn. But even after burning, they would still continue walking.

Once Jack put significant distance to the property, he stopped and turned around to face his home one final time. The flames now gyrated higher than the house itself, engulfing it entirely in orange. It pained Jack to see the farm that he and Linda started building their lives on burning into nothingness, but he had no regrets. The farm existed so that Linda and Jack could live on it, and without Linda, there could be no farm. Burning the farm down was his way of letting Linda go.

The undead had reached the property and started pouring in through the open gate and piling on the fence, rattling it. The ones who entered the house caught on fire before disappearing through the front door. A loud collapsing sound came from somewhere in the house.

Jack stared at the flames as they danced against the night sky. He looked at his hand where the wedding bands were.

My love for you is eternal.

He turned around and started walking in the direction of Cloverdale.

THE END

For all of you who are curious about the story Jack was reading to Linda – turn the page!

THE WITCH OF THE WOODS

Boris Bacic

Chapter One

There once was a boy named Will and a girl named Zara. Will and Zara were best friends who spent every day together, all day. They lived near the woods, but they never entered the woods, because the evil Witch lived there.

Chapter Two

Will and Zara went to pick berries. They spent hours putting all sorts of colorful and sweet-tasting berries in the basket. They had so much fun doing so, that they lost track of time. It was getting late, and they needed to go back home. But they would need to go around the forest to get home. "No," Will said. "We can cut through the woods."

"Golly gosh, Will," Zara said. "Through the woods? But the evil Witch lives there!"

"We have to go through the woods, because night is approaching. We will be quick! We'll be home before you know it, Zara!" Will promised.

Chapter Three

Will and Zara entered the forest. The forest was dark and filled with scary sounds, and the children stuck close to each other. Whenever Zara told Will to go back, he assured her that they would be okay in the forest. But they were not okay. They ran in circles, running into the same rocks and same trees over and over, lost in the forest. They didn't even know how to go back anymore. The sun had almost set, and Will and Zara would soon be trapped in the forest at night – when the scary monsters come out.

Chapter Four

"Gosh, Will! What should we do?" Zara asked, scared for her life.

"I don't know," Will said, also scared.

Growling came from somewhere in the forest, and eyes stared at them from the trees. Will and Zara jumped into each other's arms, ready to accept their doom. Just when they thought a dangerous monster would jump out and eat them, they heard a voice.

"I can help you," someone said.

An old woman stepped out in front of Will and Zara. They knew who she was. She was the Witch of the woods.

Chapter Five

The Witch offered to help Will and Zara find a way back. "I can help you," she said. "But you have to give me something in return." Zara asked Will to go because she knew how dangerous the Witch was, "We'll find our own way back, thank you," she said, much to the Witch's anger. But the witch warned them of the dangers in the forest. "Scary things come out at night and eat children, especially ones as cute as you," she said. Zara and Will froze. The woods grew darker with each passing second. "We'll give you want you want, just help us get back home," Will said. The Witch smiled in satisfaction. "I want your soul."

Chapter Six

The children thought for a moment. They knew that didn't have a lot of time. Without hesitation, Will agreed to surrender his soul to the Witch. "Splendid!" The Witch danced with a maniacal cackle. She told Will to put out his hand, and when the hag touched him, he felt something happening. The Witch pulled her hand back and had a bright ball in her palm – Will's soul. "Very well, I will show you how to get home," The Witch said, pointing a crooked finger in one direction while not taking her eyes off Will's soul.

Chapter Seven

True to her word, the Witch showed them the right way home. Zara rejoiced, but Will didn't seem to care. In fact, it soon became clear that Will was not the same boy that Zara knew. He no longer seemed to enjoy when the two of them played. He rarely looked at Zara. He never laughed. The Witch had led them home, but at a heavy cost. Zara wanted her friend back. She could not be happy as long as he was not happy.

Chapter Eight

Zara went back to the woods. She found the Witch and asked for Will's soul back. The Witch agreed, but under one condition – Zara would need to forfeit her own soul. But Zara knew that giving up her soul would solve nothing. She offered souls of many children to the Witch. "Many souls, you say? How?" the Witch asked.

"There is a secret place where all the children play. I will take you to them, but I want Will's soul back in return," Zara said.

The Witch, hungry for the souls of the children, agreed.

Chapter Nine

Zara led the impatient Witch toward the secret place where all the children play. The entire journey there, the Witch kept asking Zara where that place was. "You'll see," Zara said. When they finally arrived, Zara pointed and said, "Over there."

Eager, the Witch pushed Zara out of the way and stepped forward, stopping in front of a tall cliff. She realized too late that no such secret playground existed. Zara pushed the Witch, and the Witch fell from the cliff, screaming and cursing Zara before finally hitting the bottom and dying.

Chapter Ten

Zara returned to the cabin where the Witch lived. She found Will's soul, and the souls of all the children the Witch duped. Zara freed all the souls. The souls flew back to their owners, and Zara ran home to check on her friend.

When she returned, Will was smiling. He was back to his old self. They hugged and danced and played. Other children joined them soon, the ones who had their souls taken by the Witch.

With the Witch of the woods gone, the children spent many, many days playing together in the woods.

About Boris Bacic

Boris Bacic is a prolific author who has been writing stories for years, ranging from genres like horror, sci-fi, mystery, thriller, and suspense, several of them becoming bestsellers. He has been praised widely as an author who constructs compelling narratives and plots that will keep you at the edge of your seat. His stories regularly find their way among the top posts on Nosleep and he's had dozens of his stories narrated by famous Creepypasta Youtube narrators. His stories are guaranteed to make your blood run cold, give you a feeling of paranoia or make you sleep with your lights on, but will also get you attached to the characters, making you feel like you're right there with them in their predicament.

Other BDP books by Boris Bacic

Beautiful Tragedy - A Halloween Anthology
Terrifying Love - A Halloween Anthology
Just a Bite
The Witch of the Woods

www.ingramcontent.com/pod-product-compliance
Lightning Source LLC
Chambersburg PA
CBHW012014110726

47993CB00009B/3056